POULTON-LE-FYLDE
TEL: 89

D0810111

SKELMERSDALE

CTION RESERVE STOCK LL 60

0 MAR

YOU MAY RENEW YOUR
BOOKS BY PHONE: 892013

Josie Barnard was born in 1963 in New England. Soon after, her family moved back to England and settled in Yorkshire. Since moving to London in 1986 she has built a career as journalist, radio broadcaster and editor. She has contributed to a wide range of travel and literary books and wrote the Virago travel guides to London (1994) and New York (1993). She lives in north London.

POKER
FACE

Josie Barnard

Published by VIRAGO PRESS Limited 1996
20 Vauxhall Bridge Road, London SW1V 2SA

A CIP catalogue for this book is available from the
British Library

Typeset by Keystroke, Jacaranda Lodge,
Wolverhampton
Printed in Great Britain by Cox & Wyman Ltd,
Reading, Berkshire

06710467

for JMB

"**B**ugger this for a lark," our mum said. "I've had enough."'

Yes. This is satisfactory. It is printed in my best hand, in my orange Junior School exercise book. I am pleased.

It is my turn next to read out to the class.

If only *all* the school's fourteen children weren't in this one class.

I tighten my cross-legged position so that my heels lever me, straight-backed, higher slightly than the others, defiant. The classroom feels as cold to me as a disused, falling-down barn. I close the exercise book in my lap and press my hands flat over the title: *My Summer Holiday*.

I wrote it like Miss Spinkster said: as it happened.

Dawn Crawley is reading to the class now. Miss Spinkster, sitting on her heavy wood chair near the front, has the serene look on her face that makes her head tilt slightly sideways and her mouth crease a fixed smile into her mask of pink powder. Her mask will crack with extra smiling for my essay. Porky Dawn Crawley is simpering about the day she baked mud pies.

1

'The next day, I went up in my treehouse.'

She doesn't have a treehouse. She is mentioning every single thing Miss Spinkster suggested when she outlined how we could do the project. My essay is the *truth*.

I am representing our family. I know Max has a blank page in front of him, and Phyll's page is decimated.

At home, Phyll gripped the pen – *my* pen – like it was something she hated. She cut zig-zags of ink across the page then *spat* and rubbed it with her fist.

Max tugged at Dad's sleeve. 'Help me with my essay, help me.' Dad's face contorted as if someone had scraped their nails down a blackboard.

All they had to do was write.

Here in the shoolroom, Porky Dawn Crawley has come to the end of her essay.

'Then it was bedtime,' she says, shifting on to just one foot. 'The End.' She squeaks the toe of one patent leather shoe into the arch of the other, nervous, I can tell, because her whole essay was a cheat. Now she's finished, the class waits silently for Miss Spinkster's reaction.

I wriggle my collar-bone under my dungaree straps. Porky Crawley, fast turning a hawthorn-berry, shiny, red colour, hardly dares look up.

But Miss Spinkster seems delighted. Porky Dawn Crawley is being sent to sit back down with a clasping of hands and a sing-song of effusive praise. I scrutinise Miss Spinkster's pink powder mask. I conclude that this enthusiasm is a good pretence.

It is my turn to read now.

This year, I'm not sure why, I am looking forward to telling what happened in my summer holiday.

Quickly, I finger one of the big red buttons at my shoulder that keeps everything in place. I don't manage to stand entirely without shakiness, but I will not let this stop me, nor Max, who bashes his shoulders against me while hunching down into a low sulking position. I bash back. It's not *my* fault he'll have to wait even longer for Miss Spinkster's attention. I step away from him over Phyll. I would like to see *her* react, but the fringe she's grown into a matted screen is secure over her face as usual.

I am glad I elastic-banded my short hair into ponytails. It pulls my eyes taut open so I can see more clearly.

I step on towards the side of the classroom, along the row of children, past Porky Crawley's sister Karen, who shifts her knee just as my brown T-bar shoe is coming down, making me nearly trip. I stretch my leg quickly further, towards the space by Dan Pickering, see-sawing, to catch hold of his birds'-nest hair for balance. But before his hand gets near to push me, I'm away, steadying myself briefly on the radiator.

'Come on, dear,' I hear Miss Spinkster sing out. She encourages me with a friendly frontwards wave.

Sunlight is pouring in, glittering the specks of dust caught swirling in its shafts. I am hypnotised, feeling it would be possible to float up in the shafts and out, towards the sun. I force myself to walk on.

'By the blackboard,' she reminds me. I had not forgotten. I arrive there too fast.

I swivel to face into the room, but I keep my head high, aimed at the eaves where nets of cobwebs strung between the black beams are dotted with stiff cocooned prey. Spiders spin on threads that my eyes follow downwards. I glance quickly at Paul Cragg at the back, sat making fishing-flies, being too self-contained for comfort. I block him out. I concentrate totally on how the book feels gripped between my fingers, until I am safe, looking into its pages. The soles of my shoes are firm on the ground; my arms, straight in front of me, keep the book motionless in the air.

Miss Spinkster scrapes her chair minutely and makes a hollow 'hkeh' sound into her neatly furled hand. 'Start whenever you're ready,' she says, as near to impatient as she gets. I won't be hurried. I announce carefully: '*My Summer Holiday*.' My voice doesn't even quaver.

'*"Bugger this for a lark," our mum said.*'

Me and Phyll had been on the floor by the sink whisper-fighting over whose turn it was to push and whose to ride the blue tin train. Max was saying to Mum to tie his shoelaces. Dad had his briefcase on the kitchen table, keeping himself closed off from whiney bickering by looking through files. Then Mum took a step backwards; her hands turned into white-knuckled fists.

'*"I've had enough."*'

She hadn't quite said simple sentences like that, but I had to cut it up because I can't remember everything. The way her face went livid with hatred made the sounds go funny in my ears.

Vaguely I hear a more agitated 'hkeh' sound from a far away Miss Spinkster. I fill up the classroom with my voice.

'*She kicked the blue tin train.*'

Mum had been angry before, but only with her words. That day it was different.

'*"You're millstones round my neck."*'

Dad didn't move at all.

'*"I'm leaving."*'

I had still been on what she'd said before. 'Millstones?' I wanted to say, 'What do you mean?' I wanted to make her come back and explain. I looked to Dad to help me understand. But he was bent rigid over his briefcase.

I try to catch Max's eye now, to smile at him, because it feels so good to be describing everything clearly. But he is squinting slightly worse. Scrunched up on the floor next to him, Phyll has her two fingers and thumb rammed further in her mouth.

"*'There's got to be more to life than this.*'"

A spittled essay-paper pellet pinged by Ollie Ogden misses Dan Pickering and hits my leg. Why isn't he concentrating on my reading? Miss Spinkster should exert her authority, not just sit there pulling at the bobbles on her green skirt.

"*'I want a divorce*,'" I read out, louder. Suddenly Miss Spinkster stands faster than I thought she could move. She is too pleased with my work to remain sitting. She is almost shouting, 'Enough!'

Enough?

One hand goes to her neck brooch, twitching at it wildly.

'Allie,' she says in a voice that is warbling lower than it should, 'that's enough for now.'

But I worked so long. I open my mouth to start another sentence.

'Sit!' says Miss Spinkster, sharp and dizzy-looking both at once.

Ollie Ogden sneers at Porky Crawley; Dan Pickering pokes her with a compass.

I try to indicate with a sharp nod of my head to Phyll and Max that they should put a *stop* to all this disruption. But they are refusing to look at me. Karen Crawley is pushing at me to get me to go away from the blackboard.

My eyes start flitting helplessly round the growing chaos of the classroom for support. None, none, none – except in the far corner, I think I catch in the awkwardness of Paul Cragg's eyes something like sympathy.

That does it. The unexpectedness of it. I feel my legs crumpling inside my dungarees.

I sit down right where I am. I know it's not appropriate to be this close to the essay reader's feet. I stretch   **5** my chin up as far as it will go, to keep the blurring in my eyes from falling down my face.

By concentrating hard on Karen's words I can distract myself. I brace my hands against the floor. Karen Crawley is telling us how she helped her Dad milk the cows, baked cakes with her mum, made daisy chains . . .

I can't help it, turning my head. Miss Spinkster's eyes are screwed tight, tight shut. Karen's words about dressing dolls and playing skipping are not enough.

The door opens. It's Mrs Holmes the dinner-lady. Her huge shape is immediately comforting.

She is propelled forwards by her fast rotating shoulders. She will make everything all right.

Miss Spinkster whispers to Mrs Holmes. We hear, 'Please, take them away!' She is pointing in mine and Max's and Phyll's direction.

This is awful and confusing to me. Why do we have to go? My essay's stopped now.

Mrs Holmes grabs mine and Phyll's hands and bulldozes Max towards the door with her stomach. We have to do running steps to keep up as she rotates us rapidly across the boys' playground. She stops in the middle for no reason I can see, stabbing her hands furiously into her hips. We stare up at her, all of us bewildered.

It seems from her muttering it's my fault mainly. I ruined Miss Spinkster's essay session. And now Mrs Holmes has to drive us all the way home.

Well, where we live's hardly *my* fault! We didn't *ask* to get sent home.

I thought school would be better.

I hate my essay. I SCRATCH the cover with my nails. I will RIP it, SHRED it . . .

Suddenly Mrs Holmes's huge hand scoops me into her warm side. She draws Max and Phyll towards her other leg. I can smell washing-up liquid and school dinner. I clutch into the folds of her dress; squash the material hard into my eyes.

Mrs Holmes moves on towards her van, slowly now, because I've collapsed all my weight on to her, clinging.

Mrs Holmes pushes us gently into the van.

I can't even wait long enough for her to get properly into the driver's seat before I grasp again a fold of her dress. The sound of the engine drowns out everything.

This is *my* walk. I'll leave Max and Phyll behind in the house. I don't care whether they'll be all right. The afternoon sun has come out for me.

It is nearly too bright. In the yellowy fields every unevenness is lit brightly on one side. The clumps and tussocks stick out of the earth like grassed teeth, teeth that bit dead the black plank fences where they end in nowhere.

Ahead of me, the edges of the tarmac road are crumbling.

Shall I go up there, to the moor, to where it's endless with no shelter?

No. Here, I turn right. My feet nearly go from under me, scrambling over the tumbled-down dry stone wall.

Oak and pine branches lace together above my head. Sunlight sifting down makes the bracken around me blaze. I kick-spray fiery fallen beech leaves. Swirling up in the musky, dark-patched air, they catch in soft green fir.

I could run and run and never reach the end. I could jump so deep into the mudded stream that it'd sludge over the top of my wellies.

Slime fungus is seeping up the gnarled oak trunk that blocks my way. At my feet there is a hedgehog. Its prickles have been sagged by maggots.

7

I WANT HER TO BE BACK.

That's not how things are. Dead leaves at my feet – *they* are here. This hedgehog I will stamp and squash into the dirt . . .

Only it is disintegrated.

And the light is slipping. I must be home.

Lacerating brambles. Tripping fallen branches.

But I know my way. The wood can't get me lost. I am at the edge now.

I kick my ankle to make it walk properly. I bash my knuckles on the highest part of the dry stone wall until I have calmed down.

I have to be there in time for Dad.

I look out over the fields and fields I must walk over, that are turning dusk. The light at the horizon is too white. It makes the trees into skeletons.

■

It's been a while now since Mum left. We're not as nervous when Dad gets home.

7 p.m. Bham! The back door bursts open.

'How was work, Dad?' I ask, running to quickly close the door behind him. Phyll and Max stand to attention by the larder door.

'Bloody awful,' he says, already past the sink, nearly level with the cooker.

Bloody awful is not too bad.

I follow swiftly after, coming to a halt just as – crash! He heaves his briefcase on to the table. The old wood creaks under the weight of thick black leather; books, files and our dinner.

Off comes his coat, sleeves flailing as it's tossed without looking towards the cupboard by the door. I'll pick it up later. One of Dad's hands goes into the briefcase while the other goes up to his neck to wiggle loose his tie and all the while he's wrenching his left shoe-heel against the right shoe-toe to try and get the left shoe off.

He is very precarious. He pulls out . . . a packet of McCain frozen oven-chips. I'm pleased about that. But not with what follows: a squidged block of Cellophane containing what will be the centre piece of our dinner: limp grey-white Wall's sausages. If only he cooked them crisp brown all round, like they're supposed to be.

Instead Dad cooks them so I can elastic the skin in some places and chip away at bits of charred exploded sausage where it burnt to the bottom of the frying pan. He does his best. We try to help.

Max stands ready to receive his orders.

'Knife,' Dad says, like a surgeon during a delicate operation. Max drags a chair over to the sink, wooden legs screeching across the floor tiles, clunking at the ridges. Max hops up so he can reach the knife-rack.

'Little or big, Dad?'

'Any,' Dad says.

Twang! Max pulls a short, rusty knife off the magnetic strip and hops down.

Dad bends. Silently, calmly, he opens his hand to receive the knife. He assesses the joints and sinews of the Cellophane. He makes a neat incision. Pause – operating room heady with suspense – then relief as a quick slice opens the package.

Dad unravels the string of anaemic sausages on the table and stands back. Squashing his glasses hard into the bridge of his nose, he seems to be reaching a life or death decision. His jaw muscles tighten; his mouth narrows in determination.

'Grill.'

Ah-ha! A new cooking method. I stop my hand on its way to the pan cupboard by the cooker and re-direct it towards the grill tray. Phyll passes him a fork. Dad lays the string of sausages, still joined up, on the grill tray in a zig-zag line from one end to the other. He stabs **9** into each sausage twice, explaining in sentences broken by his work that it is . . . an important part of procedure . . . to spike sausage . . . to prevent skin bursting under heat.

Sombrely, he lays the fork down beside the grill tray. We all stare at the pale violated tubes on charred-black metal. Dad judges them to have been satisfactorily spiked. Me, Phyll and Max secretly cross our fingers that they will be better grilled than fried as – wham! Dad shoves the tray into place. He turns the heat indicator knob to FULL and says, 'I'm going upstairs to change.'

He takes giant strides out of the kitchen. Thunk-stomp, thunk-stomp.

'The rest of the dinner's in my briefcase,' Dad calls back, while yanking the tie into a noose wide enough to go over his head.

He leaves his jacket and tie behind him on the floor and starts in on his shirt buttons, now at the foot of the stairs and climbing.

I rummage in his briefcase for the third plastic packet. My eye is on Max and Phyll while I feel paper, cardboard, hardback book, then the squeak of plastic. I sigh. The plastic packages get ripped by book corners nearly every time. I peer in and see frost glinting.

Just like so many other nights, I have to tip the briefcase up to get our dinner. Little frozen green beads rattle down, bouncing off Dad's files and books on their way, tip-tapping a low, echoing chuckle.

I heave the briefcase on its side, then on its head, so all the peas come rattling out on to the table – whoops! – cascading on to the floor. Scoop them up, every one, and he'll never know. Pop them in a pan; pine-coloured oven-chips in a baking tray.

Make a note of the time. They'll be ready thirty minutes from now.

10   Phyll is OK, over by the larder, finishing off

colouring her doll's face blue. But Max under the table needs help building his road. He's just laid down the last of the wooden blocks. He clanks it down again as if this will make a tenth appear like in a conjuring trick. I explain from my position of superiority, standing by Dad's briefcase, about limited resources and working within one's means. I know I must sound very annoying. But I have seen a solution. I say he must make his road into a loop, with the table-leg as a centre-piece to perhaps represent a tree.

He says he can cope for himself and he wants a straight road, not a circle. I say tough, there are not enough bricks.

'What's that?' says Max, surprising me by stopping trying to push my hands off his building blocks. I ignore him, thinking he means the smell of burning that always happens when the oven gets switched on.

Max is still jabbing his finger towards something behind me. His squint is beginning to pull in. 'What's *that*?'

I turn. Wreaths of smoke are curling out from the stove's insides, winding round the hinges, creeping up the once-white enamel.

Dad must have shut the grill door. Remove the grill tray, quick. Whooosh! The flames blaze high and furious. They love it out in the open.

I hold the tray up and try to see if there is any sausage left to salvage. I wonder . . . If I throw a damp tea-towel over the sausages, perhaps we could just scrape off the charred bits and eat the bottom halves.

Max is suddenly all anxiety. He's scuttled out from under the table, shouting 'Dad! Dad!' It annoys me, the attention-seeking way his eyeballs swivel violently in towards the bridge of his nose. 'Dad! Dad!'

Dad is coming into the kitchen. Can't Max see, he's yawning because he's had a hard day's work?

Max rushes over to pummel Dad's leg: 'The house is on fire! Dad!'

Max should leave him alone, for my sake and Phyll's too.

Dad's yawn snap's shut. 'Oh my God!' He's wide awake suddenly. He grabs the grill tray from me, as if it was *my* fault. 'Out of the way, everyone out of the way!'

I try to remind him I had control of the situation: I suggest the damp tea-towel. Dad's yelling too loud to hear me.

Why should *I* care? I watch him disdainfully, grill tray at arm's length in front of him, face turned away, rushing across the kitchen, flames streaming over his shoulder. That is wasteful of him. He throws the whole lot in the sink. The metal clattering crash makes me flinch.

'Out of the way!,' he yells. 'Burning fat – *very* dangerous.'

Against my will, my feet are making obedient steps out of his way. The cows in the back field trot over to the window behind the sink to see what's going on. I resent them for being so casual. I am cowering smaller and smaller.

Dad is taking a wide, arcing detour around the kitchen, holding his sleeve over his mouth. He muffles, 'Watch out – *very* dangerous!' He turns the cold tap on the pan and leaps backwards. A tunnel of angry black smoke charges up to the ceiling; there's a cascading firework of burning, spluttering fat.

I am wise to be back here with Phyll and Max. The cows at the window scatter in terror.

Dad's still hollering that we *must* keep out of the way.

He'd only need to look round – what a relief he's not! – to realise we three are riveted together now, barriered behind the kitchen table. Our faces move in silent unison. We will not risk missing a single move.

12

Dad opens the window. He tries to wave the smoke out with his hands. The wind billows it back in. It lurks under the ceiling like rain clouds in the kitchen.

The cows are snorting curiously back towards the action again. Dad suddenly gets angry with them. He takes a furious step forwards, shouting at them to piss off.

Phyll nearly swallows her fingers and my stomach turns to lead as we see what's about to happen. I meant to and then forgot to clear up over by the sink earlier. Max mumbles uselessly, 'Watch out, Dad,' while Dad plants his foot right down where the cat, Leda, shat on the floor. He skids and grabs the sink. Now we daren't blink.

Dad doesn't fall. For a second he's stunned, suspended. Then he's furious.

'Where's that bloody animal?' he bellows.

Leda was our mother's cat. She's under the telephone chair, smirking. Not for long.

Dad grabs her by the scruff of her neck and sweeps her over to the neat squirt of fudge-coloured faeces. Dad shakes her white long-haired face and sticks it right in it, shouting 'DON'T DO IT AGAIN!' at her squirming body. Her ears are squashed flat against the floor. He gives a last twist. 'DON'T DO IT AGAIN!' he yells and then he strides over to the back door.

He throws her up into the dusk. It has been a close shave, but Leda got the brunt of the blame. She sails over the yard, her legs splayed, claws scrabbling. Her screeching miaoowww gets fainter as she goes and then there's a hiccup as she hits the barn wall. As she slithers down, unable to get a grip, she wails. Her wail winds round me, tight and painful. Furious, Leda streaks out of sight.

I hate Leda, but I wish I could leave too.

Dad slams the door. His hair's sticking out all over the place. His glasses are crooked; his face is bright red. **13**

We're lined up behind the table. I'm desperate to not show any emotion.

He notices us. Are we in for it, for witnessing his temper explode? His brows lift free of his eyes – in embarrassment. Words seem to somersault in his throat, causing vibrating 'ghrrumph' sounds. He flattens his hair and straightens his glasses.

'Well . . . ' he ghrrumphs. 'Well . . . house-training.'

I nod vigorously.

Max takes it into his head to complain, 'Why did you have to throw her so *hard*, Dad?' his voice starting to grate.

Thank goodness, Dad ignores him. 'Now!' Dad rubs his hands together, making himself suddenly cheerful. His eyebrows go firm down again, but he is looking from under them conspiratorially.

'What shall we have for dinner?' he play-asks. 'Fish-fingers?' No. The freezer compartment is empty. 'In that case,' he says. Max and Phyll wriggle excitement; I can't dare to hope . . .

Dad says, 'It'll have to be Harry Ramsden's.' We cheer! The best fish and chip shop in the North, with tablecloths and chandeliers and a framed document saying the Queen ate there!

Chairs clatter against the wall as we scramble to be quickest to the coat cupboard. Wire hangers are twanged free of macs and anoraks and we're racing from the studdering back door over the flagstones yelling, 'Me first!' 'No, me!'

Phyll gets out into the yard at a speed that comes from leg span, not effort. Max looks like a manic bantam chick, puffing his chest out to try and make his mini pin-legs go faster.

I'm not really trying, because the race is about excitement, not who goes where in the car. That's set on days when Dad's not got his briefcase. I'm the eldest.

14 I climb into the front and click the seatbelt into place.

By the time Dad's stamped his way down the path and crunched across the gravel towards the car, we're all in that fixed staring position as if we've already been travelling for miles and miles. Phyll is settled in behind her curtain of hair with her two fingers and thumb in her mouth. Max next to her has his legs at an awkward angle because they're too short when he leans back in the seat.

It feels like even the car's excited, the way it bounces when Dad starts the engine. But excited or not, it's a Citroën Diane. It won't move fast. Dad's attempt at speedy reversing to get the car pointed in the right direction for the gate causes a confused spray of white stone chips.

Through the scattering of falling gravel I see the cat, Leda, hissing rage from under the ivy by the stone trough where she has retreated. Leda should have gone when our mother did.

She's a bloody Persian. No way will I try at all to make the best of things with her. If she's not interested in the cat food she's given, left-over peas and sogged oven-chips, then she can yowl all she likes. The more the better. I'm glad Dad hurled her.

I hope he did a quick clean-up job on the cat shit while we three were dashing to the car.

If only things went smoother for him.

He's different in the car. Maybe it's because we're quiet, rocked by the Citroën Diane. His eyebrows relax to being only a bit knotted. His head's stiff but thrust not too far forward. The air inside the car is close to peaceful.

I badly don't want to get stuck behind a tractor, or for it to rain suddenly heavier than the wipers can cope with, because then Dad turns cross. Whatever's at fault, he rams his forearm at the windscreen and rubs furiously as if that way he can erase the misting up and the problem both at once. The creases of his frown 15 deepen across his forehead into black gashes lashed in multiple knots between his eyebrows.

But tonight the drive's easy.

Even though it's nearly dark I know what I would be seeing as clearly as if it was daylight. Here, at the brow of the hill, if I looked back, there would be our house – a plain granite fortress with four windows. Behind is five wire-grass fields, then the moor, which we're barricaded from by clumps of gorse. In front of the house, the moss-soft land slopes gently to the brow of the hill, and then suddenly goes steep and slippery; my ally, as if, like me, it wants to stop anyone from the village coming near.

I wonder what Dad's thinking. But I can't ask.

The main thing is, now his hands are almost loose on the steering wheel.

We're getting close. It's not echoey darkness on either side any more. The car headlights are nearly not needed because of the orange sentry streetlamps. House lights glow through curtains like we're driving into a massive set of multicoloured Christmas tree decorations. And there it is, 'Harry Ramsden's', written up in bulbs all along the flat concrete roof.

Max has fallen sideways into a wheezing half-sleep; Phyll elbows him awake.

Out on the car-park, Phyll elbows Max again, a quick jab of excitement. I reach up and grab hold of Dad's jacket while I jump up and down as fast as I can.

Dad puts one controlling hand firm on my head and one on Max's to clamp us still. His rounding palm and fingers are warming.

With my head pinioned, my vision is filled mainly by Harry Ramsden's shiny mottle-tiled front steps. Roll my eyeballs straining right up and I can see that we are equidistant between the restaurant and self-service sections: glittering chandeliers through the draped **16** curtains on my left, strip lights to my right.

I twizzel my head round under Dad's hand, so he can *feel* that I'm facing the chandelier restaurant section. I imagine how it will be to have a woman in a frilly-aproned outfit curtsey down to take the orders with a special smile then twirl back again to offer complicated ice-cream sweets for afters.

Dad has released me and is striding swift towards self-service. I don't mind, not very much. This next-door section has an atmosphere like it's a holiday outing. It's as if we're at picnic tables, sitting with our coats still on. There might not be ice-cream to eat here, but the colours are ice-cream: vanilla walls, made shiny by the fluorescent lights; chocolate flake-checked gingham uniforms behind the service counter; mint-ice table-tops that are long with slidy wooden benches attached.

Dad's gone straight to the counter without asking us what we want. I sort of wish he had, but at least this way there is a surprise. Slid into place – me, Phyll, Max – along the bench nearest the counter, we are all completely still, watching as he orders. It's nearly painful waiting. How much of a treat will it be?

Dad brings it over, his two arms loaded up awkwardly with wrapped layers and layers of paper.

A whole cod and chips *each*, and *two* polystrene half-cups steaming with sludgy green mushy peas to share between us.

The smell is wondrous – no edge of burntness, almost sticky in its richness – steaming up from the paper I'm ripping open with such glee, into my hair and clothes. I will still have the Harry Ramsden's smell all the way back in the car and maybe even a bit tomorrow.

Picking up the chips I experiment squashing three, four, five together so they collapse warmth round my fingers as I shove them into my wide-opened mouth. I break off the batter end and use it as a cup to carry two flakes of white fish up and in with the mashed chips. I glance sideways and see Max has squeezed **17** ketchup from the plastic tomato to smear it with a flat wooden spoon-fork over the crinkly brown surface of his fish. That's a good idea. Dollop mushy peas on top. Sandwich it with a layer of chips, and—

'*Don't* play with your food,' Dad says, not sharp yet. But I can't push it. My appetite is twisted by dread that he'll remember any minute now that we've got school tomorrow.

I try to stay absorbed in my feast while keeping half an eye on him. One shoulder's by his ear while he scrabbles about in his pocket for a pencil stub and an old receipt, which he's using as a scrap of paper to make a list on.

We're eating fast. He's only got through half his dinner and now he's taken out his work diary. At least he hasn't got the car keys out yet.

I weigh up between preferring the fish so wanting to leave it till last but being determined not to get dragged away when I've only eaten chips. I make a compromise: fish, chips, fish, chips – and succeed in getting it all down within split seconds of Max and Phyll finishing theirs.

Dad's practically out at the car. We're wiping our hands on our coats as we scamper after him.

My stuffed-full stomach's uncomfortable against the seatbelt. But I'm satisfied, being shaken by the Citroën, gently shaken, my eyes pulling themselves closed. Try to stop them; stare at the sentry street-lights to keep myself awake. Not often we're allowed to stay up late. The lights flick past, and past. Starting to merge. Orange streamers, waves of orange streamers to celebrate that we've been out. Been treated. Orange streamers. Streamers.

Mint, vanilla, chocolate ice-cream.

18　　　'Allie.'

My mummy is calling to me softly through the streamers. I heap mint, vanilla and chocolate ice-cream on to a big silver spoon.

'Allie.'

A different voice is crashing through the streamers. My hand is cold.

'Allie.'

It is Dad, trying to wake me gently. But his voice won't come out quiet.

I lurch out of the car door and stagger on to the gravel.

Max is slung over Dad's shoulder. All that's left for me to hold on to is his jacket hem. Even through sleep haze, I feel a stab of resentment at Max for being more than his fair share of burden on Dad.

At least the kitchen light being switched on shocks Max into jerking his head awake. Only now all Dad can concentrate on is getting Max to bed. *What about me*?

Guilt niggles at my brain that three arcing streaks are left on the floor where Dad used washing-up liquid to clean up the cat shit. But then I feel a knot of anger. Who does he expect to do the rest? The grill pan's where it was, crashed at an angle in the sink; bits of charcoaled dinner are stuck by blobs of congealed white fat on to the taps, the stained steel draining-board, the window.

I'm suddenly weighed down by responsibility.

Dad scissors his body down for a goodnight kiss. His cheek's level with my face for a split second. I am swamped by gratefulness.

''Night, Dad,' I mumble to the bits of him that are flicking past my eyes faster than telegraph poles flick by the car window. I concentrate on the harsh hessian weave of the stair carpet. I try to match the speed of his stomping away from me so I get myself upstairs faster. I heave myself up by the bannister. I hear Dad clinking **19** whisky into a glass downstairs. I turn round the door jamb. I enter mine and Phyll's bedroom.

Phyll is lying there staring up through her veil of hair at mid-air, her two fingers and thumb still firm in her mouth. I would like to chop off her fringe. She didn't close the curtains or anything. Her covers are pulled right up level with her chin. Her brown T-bar shoes are kicked off, getting in my way.

I'd like to complain. Usually, I can be sure if she's not asleep from the atmosphere.

If I'm wrong, though, I think, as I tiptoe a stepping-stone path across the carpet's thick-stalked leaves – if I'm wrong and I wake her, I'll get the *angry* atmosphere. As quietly as I can, I rattle the hessian curtains along the metal rail.

It's not like hessian keeps the cold out, or even as if there's any heat to keep in anyway. But I shut them because I like the way the sunlight comes through the woven threads when I wake up in the morning, turning it ruby coloured and making the whole room look warm and rich. Redness seeps into the threadbare bits of the carpet, turning it thick and glossy. Thin dun patches blossom into fairy-tale magenta trumpet flowers.

In the dark, though, like now, the trumpet flowers look like opened jaws.

I climb past the shadows of Phyll's bedstead into the shadows of my own.

It's cold. I won't undress. I jam my shoes between the mattress and the wall. The only risk is Dad finding out. He'll probably fall asleep before remembering to check on us.

I edge under the covers without untucking them. I like to feel the sheet, heavy with blankets, as tight across my shoulders as possible. I aim to lie flat all night. It doesn't stop me getting the stretchy thing, though.

Just thinking about it unsettles my stomach, knowing how it might only be one foot at first, but soon it can be my whole body that is being stretched – huge, tiny, all in different directions.

I tried to tell Dad about the stretchy thing. He didn't understand. He said to go and tell him next time it happened. But the whole point is I can't even move a finger. I tried to explain how it makes me feel. Like a huge black hole swallowing me up. He did make a big effort to see what I was talking about. He knotted his eyebrows and shoved his glasses hard into the bridge of his nose while he concentrated on looking at me. Then he combed his hand into his hair in despair that quickly turned to crossness. Everyone gets things like that, he seemed to be thinking. My eyes pricked from trying to squeeze back rage. He bashed objects about on his desk.

'Well . . . wait for it to finish and go to sleep,' he snapped at a paperweight. 'Or get up and have a glass of water,' he added, trying to sound sympathetic in the direction of a paper knife. 'Or something,' he grumbled, finally dismissing me with an impatient brush of his hand.

I'm glad we were up late tonight. I am ready for sleep. The tinny sounds of the telly creep through the floorboards from the living-room below. I kick my feet a little bit at the covers to warm up that section of air. The tinny tune changes to a deep rumble: 'Bong – Bong – Bong . . . ' The *News at Ten*. The sound makes me anxious usually, because it means it's ten o'clock and I should have been asleep long ago.

'Bong . . . '

I can feel with my back through the mattress the low buzz that is the newscaster's voice.

It is frustrating not knowing for sure if Dad is awake to hear it. I have to creep downstairs, sometimes, and sink into my swinging hunched position by **21** the living-room door. There's a split second while I get my eye to one of the cracks in the planks when I panic in case he's not there. Of *course* he is. Then I wonder if he's OK.

He starts off upright in the yellow armchair, looking like he's so much *wanting* to watch telly, his forwards-thrust face intent as if he is in an informal meeting. His head slides down the back of the chair. Even making burnt sausages and sogged oven-chips is like crawling up a mountain to him.

His hands, balanced precariously on his chest, lose their grip on the empty glass and it rolls to the floor.

When I get too cold hunched outside the living-room door, I creep back to bed, better for having an image of Dad in my head that is relaxed: the knots loosened between his brows, the tiny constant movements under the skin where he tightens, *clenches* his back teeth at last easing.

Now, along with the low buzz of the newscaster's voice, the sound creeping up is Dad beginning to snore, faint throaty rattles. Outside, the thorny rose-branches are scraping against the window. The wind is howling, trapped in the chimney. Sometimes in this house it is hard to keep things in perspective. Sounds seem to magnify, in contrast with the stretched-out silence of the moor, getting louder, *louder*. But it's not too bad tonight.

Next door, Max is shouting out in his sleep, broken phrases. His rickety bunk-bed begins to crash plaster from the wall. There is a dull, reverberating floorboard sound as his body hurtles from the top bunk.

It is a long fall. No-one goes to him. He will be bruised tomorrow and say he slept fine. His squint will be slightly worse, the quavery blue-grey irises defying us to look in both at once, then clouding over furious when Dad, then me, then Phyll won't even try.

Phyll just stays behind her curtain of hair and that's that. Has done ever since the time she complained to Mum that the fringe was getting in her eyes and Mum snapped back, 'Brush it to one side, then!'

That was when Mum and Dad were having the arguments. There was nothing to do but lie rigid in bed, eyes wide open, pretending not to hear. Finally, tears. Dad gruff, failing to comfort her. It would take ages for us to get to sleep after. The next morning they'd be surrounded with black clouds of tiredness so they wouldn't see that we had darkness under our eyes too.

Mum used to stroke my head before I went to sleep. She used to lean down and press her cheek against my cheek. She used to rock me in her arms.

But that was a long time ago.

I listen to the sounds of the house. Dust is kicked off the beams by mice in the rafters. It sounds like elephants have stampeded across the roof. I think what Benjy and Mary would do if they were up there now. They would sort those mice out.

Mary and Benjy are *our* cats. Even Dad likes them.

The mice are scurrying behind my head now. I want to bash the wall and make them go away.

Downstairs the telly is winding up to its long screech. The night's viewing is over. The screech goes on. Phyll shoves the covers off. Her feet crash to the floor and down the stairs to switch the telly off.

'Dad. It's finished,' I hear her mumble, like it's not a worry to interrupt Dad's sleep.

'What?' He does not sound pleased.

I hear Phyll click off the light. Dad's passage is marked by grrummphs as his shoulders career from side to side up the stairwell.

Soon his guttural snore will be rumbling the house. We went to Harry Ramsden's tonight. In the shadows of my bed, I smile.

Nightmare noise guns my head off the pillows. I am jiggering on the carpet like a broken clockwork soldier: know I have duties; can't think what they are.

'It's eight o'clock!'

The whine-screaming is Max – how did he get downstairs before me? It's *my* responsibility to wake everyone up.

I try to fix my eyes on grabbing my shoes from where they're stuck between the mattress and the wall. The buckle is the most difficult puzzle I have ever had to do. Think, think. Why shouldn't I have gone to bed in all yesterday's clothes?

School photograph; must look smart.

To the wardrobe.

Two flowered dresses hang in front of my eyes, mine green, Phyll's pink. They are warning. The unnatural colours fight with the tasteful white collars and cuffs. Like the way I clash at school.

I don't understand. Julie Reed manages to control the kids at our school, and she is *much* worse off than having had a mother leave.

'Bugger this for a lark,' I mimic sourly in my head. Anyway, I'm glad Mum's gone. I can control my own idea of smart.

I will squeeze my green flowered dress *on top* of my bee-stripe jumper. I *like* it that the skirt billows stupidly under the boa-constricting torso.

Only, what if the other school children, particularly Karen Crawley and Ollie Ogden, see that we are rejects?

I might burst with fury at Max's usurping, the way he's shouting from downstairs, 'It's *gone* eight o'clock!'

I kick open his bedroom door, to make it clear *I'm* having to sort out *his* smart clothes.

He might not have much stuff, but he can still make his room look like a battlefield: his duvet flapping like a flag off the top bunk; action man, head snapped backwards; mauve T-shirt in crumpled body-shape in front of the ransacked blond pine chest.

I kick his T-shirt messier. *I* shan't tidy it up.

At the back of the bottom bunk drawer I find the pink-flowered shirt with matching elasticated tie. He can't even get this right. They will be too small.

I might still get told off for him not looking smart.

'Dad! Dad!' he screams even louder, just to extra infuriate me that such a whiner is under my remit.

'We'll be late for the school bus!'

I stare from the car window hopelessly.

It is where we wait for the school bus. The Pillar: an old stone gatepost sunk in to a triangle of muddied grass. But as I shut the door behind Max and Phyll, it is like we are raw flesh.

'Bye Dad!'

Me and Max and Phyll stick closely together, waving our hands in exact time with each other to emphasise how massively we all four love each other.

Ollie Ogden is crouched on top of the Pillar. 'Ha ha!' he says, 'a rubbish Citroën Diane! *My* Dad 'as a BMW.'

Yes, and it's cream, and it gets mud-splattered by tractors going past, I think to myself.

I would like to feel snooty. But Max and Phyll are pressing closer for protection. I edge us away from Ollie towards the dry-stone wall.

Dan Pickering suddenly stops bashing his siblings. Karen Crawley fixes her eye on us in the reflection of her pink hand-mirror. Dawn Crawley begins to turn.

In the folds of my dress, my fingers cross round and round till my hand's an aching spiral.

Karen starts sniggering. I get all my jaw and forehead muscles flattening my face.

'I wonder,' she sneers, ''ow it feels ter 'ave *frog eyes*.'

Darned sight better, I rage inside my head, than to look like a pig – right down to her feet, trotters squeezed into frilled ankle socks. But I'm scrabbling shale. She turns on Phyll.

'Twig legs!'

I unbalance with panic. Once one of us reacts, we've all had it.

'Will's coming!' shouts Ollie Ogden suddenly.

My heart leaps guiltily.

''Ere 'e comes.'

Will Reed, with his thick neck and mouth hanging slightly open, lumbering down the right-hand fork. Now it is *him* who will get savaged.

'Mong!' shouts Ollie Ogden.

Will covers his eyes with his sleeve in exaggerated shyness.

'Mong, mong!'

Ollie Ogden is a wolf-mutated hobgoblin, slavering up there on the Pillar. I would like to shove him inside his own teeth.

Will is smiling – coy, confused. His humiliation has hardly begun.

Dan Pickering pushes him roughly towards Porky Dawn Crawley. 'Go on, kiss 'er. She's yer girlfriend. Do it.'

I try to tell myself that this is only group silliness. It does William no harm.

The taunting is loud. Will has to cover his ears. Dan Pickering is twisting Will's arm. I daren't move. Will cries out in pain. Karen Crawley joins in Ollie's chant:

'Mong! Mong!'

Ollie's tune changes: 'Julie's coming! Julie's coming.'

I could run and hug and kiss Julie Reed! Except, that it's obviously entirely out of the question. I back harder into the dry-stone wall.

It was stupid of Karen and Dawn and Ollie and all the Pickering boys to stay out there in the open. Julie's coming. They are forced to cower round us. I can even bear Karen's pudgy hand shoving on my knee so she can lean nonchalant. Her and Ollie and everyone are our padding.

Julie has stopped only feet away.

It is like my eyes are magnetised. I am privileged to be looking at her furious flame orange curls. Her skin is so paper-white it is intimidating. Her freckles stand out livid. But mostly, I am in amazement at her self-control.

First she is concentrating on Will, her brother.

'Yer all right?' she says softly. 'G'won. Back ter t'house then.'

Will runs – huge, oafish, obedient strides – back towards their home.

My blood lurches. Since Julie Reed never asks who's been roughing her brother, it could be any one of us she decides to pick on.

I am trying suddenly to be the lowest head. Phyll and Max, our shoulders glued, join me disappearing downwards. I make sure, though, to have a clear view between Karen and Ollie's slightly but definitely quaking necks.

I want to see everything Julie Reed does.

She has a hole in her heart. It should be her affliction.

Julie moves her hand. The group gasps.

Ah – she is only touching her chest just near where the scar shows at the top of her shirt. I would like to touch it, where the skin is impenetrable shiny. But she would never let anyone that close.

27

They had to saw through her ribcage. She is superhuman.

Right now, she is in contemplation, staring down at the tarmac cracks which sprout weeds. The extreme colour of her freckles has calmed. She lifts her head. Her eyes have narrowed. She begins to walk towards the Pillar.

We all stop breathing. Who will it be?

I begin to think maybe being embedded in the group will be taken as a sign of allegiance. My head, echoed by Phyll's and Max's, shoots up and turns towards the church steeple, distantly independent. Heart hammering, I desperately hope it's worked. Julie's eyes target . . .

Thank goodness: Porky Dawn Crawley. Julie nods to Karen Crawley to hold her down. I find I am even quite excited. I stay firm against the wall though. Karen and Ollie and the Pickerings snarl forwards.

Julie nods to Dan Pickering. I shift my shoulder blades and bum-bones to feel more comfy against the wall.

Dan rubs his hands. He circles Dawn Crawley. He stops. He makes his right hand into a fist and places it in the flat of his left hand. He says to Dawn Crawley through the gap in his chipped front tooth, 'Smell the cheese.' Dawn leans forwards, resigned, and sniffs at his fist. He smashes it into her face.

I assess that Dawn Crawley has decided today she will not cry out. Foolish. If I was Julie, I'd want a reaction. The sooner she gets one, I'm sure, the sooner she will stop.

Dan asks how the cheese smelled, 'Huh, huh, huh.' Porky Dawn Crawley begins to snivel.

I look to Julie, waiting to see how she will be inspired. She is staring into air, her eyelids not moving. Her emerald green eyes have sparks of yellow. They can look vulnerable, or innocent. But they are hard. They probe. They are her barrier.

28

'The bus, the school bus!' Ollie informs her. My ears adjust like they are being jolted down to earth. The engine is groaning and wheezing up the hill.

The school's walls go up and up and touch the sky. This is Julie Reed's domain. Her breaktime headquarters are in the grassy corner of the playground. She is regal, sitting in the crook of the crab-apple tree. It would just take a flicker of one of her frail, freckled hands and every pupil would be at her feet, ready. Except Paul Cragg. He is already nearby, engrossed making wire-loop rabbit traps. She doesn't control him. I feel envious, and diminished, that he can be there of his own accord. The rest of us merely make pretence at being free to do our own leisure.

Ollie Ogden and Dan Pickering are involved in hushed bickering about whether they should play British Bulldog or What's the Time, Mr Wolf? Karen Crawley's got Sarah Groats and Alison Dibble positioned on either side of her, with subtle daring in the *middle* of the playground, ready for Karen to play elastics.

I am hanging like a bat from the low red brick wall. I have Max and Phyll tight in beside me. Karen turns suddenly to mouth something – 'Scruffy'? No! It is just my own style, jumper squeezed under dress. I remind myself where I am facing. My upside-down head is direct in line with Julie Reed. I bask in her power. It is absolute. Even when Miss Spinkster was actually *told* that Julie Reed bullied – and I still can't quite believe Porky Crawley did it – Julie's position was only strengthened.

I had levered up on the window-sill, riveted by Porky Crawley stranded in front of Teacher's desk. Porky Crawley had no *proof* that Julie Reed had made her stamp her crisps into the boys' toilet floor and eat them.

'I'll have to teach you once and for all,' cried Miss Spinkster, her pink face powder quivering precariously, 'that lying, especially when it implicates such a poor, afflicted girl, is wicked. Do you understand? *Wicked!*'

It may only really be a piece of rotting garden stick, not a proper cane, but normally Miss Spinkster would *never* use it. The garden stick whistled up furiously; even though it only came down with hardly enough energy to tickle Porky Crawley's upturned hand, the 'caning' was equivalent to Miss Spinkster giving total endorsement. Julie Reed can do anything she wants.

I think she sort of likes me. The only bullying she ever does on me and Phyll and Max is make us put bits of dried cowpat in our mouths. She doesn't make sure we chew or swallow. We spit it out later.

Hanging upside-down by hooking my knees over the wall, I stare with fondness at Julie, who seems from my position to be defying gravity by not falling out of the crab-apple tree into the sky. There is something reassuring about seeing everything turned wrong-side up. Karen, twanging cat's cradle configurations with her feet, looks idiotic, singing out stamping rhymes when she's bobbing elasticated from a tarmac ceiling. I am lulled by her shouting – 'I like coffee' (stamp), 'I like tea' (stamp), 'I like sitting' (stamp), 'On a man's knee' (stamp). As long as that carries on, we are safe.

Her elastic-stamping's stopped.

The underneaths of my knees are sore from hanging on the wall. My skirt's flapping ungainly round my chest.

Karen's coming over, *while Julie's there.*

Ollie and Dan and Dawn and Sarah and Alison are in pack formation.

If Julie noticed, everything would be OK. They'd have to stop.

'Wharr are they?' Karen incisors. 'They're *The*

Three Scruffy's.' With full snarling conviction that she's gnawing into bone: '*The Three Scruffy's!*'

I would like to be smashed into a thousand screaming pieces.

'*The Three Scruffy's!*'

The school door opens. Miss Spinkster swings the handbell. Metal clappering from side to side clangs away the nightmare.

I am surrounded by irritating children.

Miss Spinkster gives extra swings to the bell.

I am being hustled. The other pupils are elbowing and kneeing faster than the pace I want. I hate this bleach-stinking passage! It is like the school wants to disinfect me. I squeeze my nostril muscles together.

But, wait – should Max and Phyll be slightly ahead or behind for me to give them most protection? I try to grapple hold of bits of their clothing. They are being taken out of my control. I needle a finger sharp into Dan Pickering's side from an angle that will make him think it was Ollie Ogden. He turns in oafish aggravation. I dart past.

I'm clear through the gaping high doorway. I have got Phyll and Max secured at my sides. We are so firmly linked we could have a metal lynchpin through the three of us. We stand ram-rod straight, in front of the orange nylon-covered blackboard backdrop. Because, out of everything that is earthquakingly uncertain, I know that we will be photographed first. We are 'B' for 'Bennett'.

That is one thing we have over all the other children. Alphabetical supremacy.

Knowing we'll soon be finished, I can face the school photographer with defiance – if he will only look up from fiddling behind his tripod camera's black cloth.

While there is a gap before I have his attention, I brush my hair very carefully with the flat of my hand. I brush and brush so that even the back goes tight to my head.

Delicately, I remove my bee-stripe jumper. I can't help smiling at the bold garishness of my dress, the way it is spattered with green flowers. It clashes spectacularly with Phyll's matching luminous pink one and especially with the delicate design of Max's pastel-design floral shirt.

Children are scattered randomly over the scuffed parquet floor beyond the photographer. They are absorbed in games of jacks and spillikins. This is good. We are of no consequence.

I am avoiding Miss Spinkster's eye, because I know she is avoiding mine. The casual chat she is having about weather with the photographer comes over to me like wafting stringed insults. We are the photographer's subjects. We ought to be the objects of her concentration.

At last. The photographer is out from his cloth, doing his hands in a square to frame us up. It's like my body is being strained in conflicting directions, I am so ready to do whatever he will instruct us. He commands me and Max on to a small chair each, Phyll to stand behind.

OK. He wants a loving family group. I can do that. I grasp on to Max's fingers. He is fidgeting them away, as if it is embarrassing to be seen in public holding his big sister's hand. This is childish of him. But I must be considerate.

I don't have time. The photographer's yanking a strand of hair across his balding head, to declare impatience.

I shove my arm up over the back of the chair so me and Phyll can hold hands instead. But she won't take her right hand out of her mouth. Her left is flopped on Max's shoulder. I suppose that will have to do.

I smile my biggest smile. The photographer suggests that Max and Phyll smile too.

Why do they have to wait for him to say so? It's *obvious* that's what they're required to do. I smile even bigger. I see out of the aching corner of my eye that Max is at least changing his expression, but all that's happening is his squint's going in, making him look more cross. Is he trying to spite me?

This delay is leaving Ollie and Dan boredom-space to throw the rubber ball and swipe the jacks more and more disruptively. Miss Spinkster is emitting a strangulated *shhshing* sound.

Mrs Holmes is bustling in with a cup of tea for the photographer, who is now distinctly irritated.

She throws her hands up in horror. 'Yer hair,' she says. I glare at Phyll. I knew it. Obviously, there's no point taking a photo of a child you can't see because their fringe is grown matted over their face. Phyll will have to brush it . . .

So what's Mrs Holmes's hand doing on *my* fringe, tugging? Get off! I reel my head back. I'm not one of those dolls with hair you can grow and style. It's meant to be like this. It's my Dad's haircut. He couldn't get it straight the third, or fourth time. But it doesn't get in my eyes.

I want to smash away the prodding index finger that's spittling the stubbled fringe into my hairline. My forehead's sticky. Mrs Holmes turns to deal with Phyll, and I rub it dry with the back of my hand. I like my fringe! I make what little there is stick up.

And Mrs Holmes has no right to touch Phyll's hair. Good on Phyll, for getting her hand out of her mouth just long enough to fend Mrs Holmes off, before she puts them straight back in again. Ha!

Mrs Holmes is panting. She is red-faced, defeated, glaring at Phyll who is standing quietly behind Max again.

'Into the kitchen,' she says. 'Both of you.'

This is too much, dragging me forcibly. Mrs Holmes is Chinese-burning my wrists. My digging heels won't get a grip. I throw my head backwards, pleading with my eyes for Phyll to follow. Phyll grips her chair harder.

I tell myself it is only imagination that I hear *Scruffy! Scruffy!* as I am wrenched out round the door jamb.

Squashed in by yellow kitchen units, I wish Mrs Holmes would just pulverise me into oblivion. That would be kinder.

'We'll get those creases out, iron, or no iron. We'll steam 'em out,' she says, turning up the gas to boil the kettle.

My dress, and I'd put it on with such conviction.

'Lift your arms.' She pulls the dress over my head.

It's like I am in shock, doing everything she tells me.

'Cover yourself wi' these.' She hands me three tea-towels. She holds my dress over the steam-spouting kettle. She mutters to herself. 'Jus' look at t'state o' it . . . I s'pose t'father can't be blamed . . .'

Does she think I'm deaf? I would tell her that my Dad is bloody brilliant – except it is a struggle getting these tea-towels anywhere near to covering me up. I put the one that has a picture of Fountains Abbey across my chest. I clamp it in place with my armpits. I swallow hard. I drape York Minster over my shoulders. Fountains Abbey slips down my chest. I pull it up. I swallow harder. I try and get the Dales of Yorkshire over my legs.

There is sniggering at the crack of the kitchen doorway. Salt water hydraulic-powers up the back of my throat. Dan Pickering's eyeballs are staring snideness over Ollie Ogden's over Karen Crawley's. I can't pretend. They are hissing the 'Scruffy' chant.

I stretch my eyebrows so high and my mouth so wide and my ears so far apart and my chin so far down that even if there are welling tears, my face will look too contorted for it to be possible to tell.

More vicious sniggering.

Mrs Holmes declares, 'Shoo!'

About time. They scamper. Salt water is pounding round my head, but at least it's not coming out.

''Ere you are, dear,' says Mrs Holmes. 'Good as new.'

It's not new. It's ancient. It's too small. I preferred it creased.

It doesn't feel right anymore.

'Off you go,' says Mrs Holmes, pushing me back into the classroom. 'And give t'photographer a nice big smile.' I've forgotten how.

When we get sent home early, I come to Fairy Dell.

I on purpose never ask where Phyll and Max go. If we were *supposed* to be off school, perhaps it would be different – maybe we would wreak havoc in the kitchen. But we aren't. And we can't tell Dad about it later.

There's all sorts of things we can do wrong and he only gets a bit annoyed. Like breaking a plate is a minor inconvenience. But missing school . . .

So when we get home I come down to Fairy Dell. I especially don't tell Dad I've been here.

The thought of him finding out makes me want this piece of dirt I'm stood on to gape open and drag me in suffocating.

Fairy Dell was where we all used to come. We would have picnics. They would lie together on the gingham cloth, paper plates and left-over sandwiches spilling into emerald green grass and gracefully nodding bluebells. Me, Max and Phyll would make paper boats to float in the stream, or try running down the bank on the other side as fast as we could without touching any of the clumps of sunshine yellow wild primroses.

Today Fairy Dell is all dead pine trees and the smell of rotting.

I sit on a stone and shove at the bank of the stream with my feet until lumps of earth and bracken collapse, filthying the water. I don't care that my posh dress is getting streaked dirty. With a stick, I dab mud into the centres of its radiation-luminous flowers, which look pathetic in what little light can fight through twisted black branches.

Sometimes a picnic would become a party. Together they had lots of friends. Dad's friend Bernard used to come. One time the atmosphere wasn't as it should have been. Plastic cups of wine got downed in one. There was no relaxed sipping.

Bernard took my hand and started walking off into the bluebells. He told me that I looked like a fairy starting on a warpath, I should take care. I said, stupid. Fairies don't exist.

He galumphed beside me, gone silent and into himself, just holding my hand. Now I know he was comforting me in advance. I got mixed up. I thought he wanted cheering up. I told him jokes.

He was the only one who overlapped even for a while after Mum left. He was like an oak tree I could cling to.

Him and Dad work together. Bernard was Dad's closest friend. One day Bernard turned-up unexpectedly. I don't know how he dared. The probability that Dad was working at his desk was ominously high. Dad did make a special effort to pretend he didn't mind being interrupted.

Bernard bellowed out 'Martin!' as heartily as always. But as he clapped Dad on the back fit to wind him, Bernard was tugging uneasily at his curling-up Edward Lear beard. I waited, face upturned, eager. But he didn't have special words of flattery and jollity for us three.

'Martin, why don't you show me round your *beautiful* garden,' he bellowed with a hollow expansive gesture. I should've told him, his attempt at tact was hopeless. It was clear to all of us that he wanted to have a talk with Dad.

I didn't mean to, really, but I ended up round by the stone trough. I heard the front door pulled shut as they came out into the garden. I didn't want them to see me through the garden gate in the wall and think I was spying. I crept under the ivy and sunk into my hunched swinging position. I couldn't help hearing.

'I've known you for a long time, Martin.'

The hugeness of Bernard elephanting across the grass made the ground beneath my feet thunder.

'I knew you both.'

The thunder was cut short. I didn't have to see to know Dad's eyebrows had knotted so tight his eyes were covered over completely.

Bernard knew Dad better than most people, but he carried on.

I swung my hunched body faster between my bent-up legs.

'This must be a difficult time for you, Martin. But for God's sake, ease up – for the children if not for yourself.

'You've got to talk about how you're feeling to someone. I'm *worried* about you, Martin. You've made yourself so hard, you're going to crack!'

There was silence. I was fooled by idiotic hopes, of warmth that would wrap me round.

Dad's 'Thank you, but I really must be getting back to work now' sounded bitter. I rammed my knuckles on the feelingless cobbles.

Bernard galumphed, defeated, back to his car in the yard.

That was the last time I saw him. Dad made us answer the telephone after that. He has no close friends now. Hardly anyone comes to the house.

It's getting dark. It's time for me to go home.

Maybe Dad will notice that my dress is ruined. Perhaps he will ask how the school photograph went.

I know he will be tired and irritable. Max will try and fail to get attention. Phyll will remain angrily removed from us all. And I shall feel weary all evening, then not be able to get to sleep.

■

Today I am ill. Every so often it becomes necessary.

Symptoms aren't a problem. I only have to not splash cold water on my face in the mornings and the blackness from not sleeping stays all around my eyes. Then I let the stretchy thing take over – my panic looks like pain.

The key is not so much the symptoms as the timing. The only day Dad will even consider allowing us to be ill is Mondays, when Mrs Taylor comes.

This suits me very well. It's not just needing to extricate myself from the way school squashes my head like a cranking metal vice; Mrs Taylor has some answers.

Today went smoother than clockwork. I felt a guilty twisting of my insides that Dad let me off so quickly. He must have felt desperate too, only all he got was a missed first hour of work.

When I forced myself to blurt out a warbly, 'Dad, I don't feel well,' he did grind his jaw, but then he didn't do the call-the-doctor threat to try and double-bluff me.

38   I felt a coward and a cheat when he brought a

slice of bread and cheese upstairs. He could have spent that time on a paragraph, maybe even reading a whole page. As he placed my plate on the floor, his eyes looked more bashed up than mine must do. He examined me so caringly, I had to turn away.

Then I stared back, quickly. His arms came round to cocoon me in a blanket. I seemed shrunk to when I was a tiny infant, when he used to muck about and play that I was a present which he was wrapping up.

I didn't have to walk. He carried me, down all the stairs, out to the car. I knew I shouldn't have, because of being 'ill', but I clung to his neck when he was trying to bundle me in the back. He eased my fingers off. This cocooning was for a purpose.

We are collecting Mrs Taylor.

Mrs Taylor has known us since before we were born. She has a helmet of silver hair; just thinking of it makes me feel protected. She's stuck by us. Despite everything. Even after we moved out here.

It is a whole hour extra travelling for her, plus a two and a quarter mile walk, uphill, from the bus-stop to our house.

But today, and I can take the credit – it is because of me being ill – she doesn't have to walk.

Her bus must be nearly at the iron bridge stop by now. The Citroën's wheels go in ruts and over tarmac clumps. In the back seat, I am bounced into excitement. I got Dad to let me off school! It's becoming hard to keep up the storm-cloud facial symptoms. Dad colluded with me. I hoik the cocoon blanket up practically to my hairline to stop the smirks escaping.

As the car turns at the bottom of the hill and we drive along by the river, it is a relief that I can concentrate on seeing Mrs Taylor. She steps down from the bus. She sets on the pavement her leather-look shopper. Its big handles and mysterious depths make me think of Battenburg and fairy-cakes. I feel my eyes are sparkling in anticipation of, maybe, gratitude. She'll see us coming, any minute.

She is taking out from her shopper a pink polyester scarf. She folds it in half neatly. I wonder at her preciseness, which is so opposite to us. She places the triangle on her head, high over her helmet of silver hair, and secures the scarf with a knot under her chin. I would be running trying to do everything at once. She swiftly buttons her light grey mac; she hangs the shopper in the crook of her arm and marches over the iron bridge.

Now, unexpectedly, I am starting to feel uncomfortable. I don't think Mrs Taylor would ever allow herself to be ill. I have let her down. She will see right through me.

I sink below the front-seat line. I am too anxious about her response to risk missing it completely, though. I peer upwards. I will be able to see a section of her face; she might not notice me, entrenched.

The car pulls to a stop beside her. The door slams.

From down here in the car-plasticked smell of mud and wellies, her silver hair rises in a spiralling halo. I periscope my head to work out where she's looking. Relief! Her scouring eyes are completely on Dad. I slide back up the seat. While finding and pulling the seat-belt into place, she's examining his face. I wind my arms into the blanket edges and make taut the protection round myself. I feel almost smug. I know what Mrs Taylor's looking for: blackness of mood.

I glance over at Dad's knuckles on the steering wheel and I know beforehand what I'll see. They are not stretched completely white from tension. I feel proud of my achievement. He's had an extra three quarters of an hour of placating work-time at his desk at home, because of me. I know from the way lines are fanning into Mrs Taylor's temples that she's smiling as she
leans back.

But I've been too cocky. 'Allie,' she says in her most provocative Scottish lilt; I'd like the back car door to eject me, 'you're a touch peaky today, then?'

My stomach radiates quivering that rattles even the hardness of my nails. It is hollow comfort that the blanket is covering the fact that I am blushing.

It's not fair that she can make me do the thing I'm practising to eliminate. Mrs Taylor tweaks her scarf edges exactly into place. I try to make the blood drain out of my face back to furious-pump my heart.

But even while I feel I might be succeeding, I notice with dismay, her fan-lines have gone. From the direction of her gaze it's clear, for the moment I am irrelevant to her. A hiccup of hurt is subdued by panic.

We're turning into the yard. Last Monday's washing is still flapping on the line.

How can I not see these things till Mrs Taylor's here? We should have put it all away – *I* should have.

She shakes her head, a snap-shake as if she knows she'll have cause to shake her head many more times through today. At least Dad appears to be oblivious to the humiliation of our mess. His eyes go magnetised to his wrist-watch. Mrs Taylor pulls the belt of her mac one notch tighter. 'Don't you worry, Martin,' she commands. 'Allie can manage.'

Shutting the door quieter than a mouse, I hardly dare mumble, 'Bye Dad.' Certainly, no concluding peck-kiss.

It is not difficult to affect an ill person's lope up the path. I doubt if Dad is noticing that the blanket is trailing pathetically behind as he spray-gravel reverses out of the yard. But there is an outside chance. I bow my head. Then, as soon as he's gone, I yank up the patchy wool swathes and run to catch up with Mrs Taylor.

Breathless, I am behind her. I stare forlornly past her pristine-pressed mac, through the back door window. The unpleasantness is clogging up my eyes.

41

Jam stickied into the table. Dried foot- and paw-prints dancing mockingly over the red-tiled floor. Cans and packages and empty bottles erupting from the swing-bin.

I can hardly force myself to face her expression.

I try to make her pleased with me. I stick my hand in front and open the door for her. I am not surprised that she doesn't thank me. I don't mind.

I find her rituals numbingly comforting.

In the centre of the kitchen, impervious, she removes her triangle of scarf and touches – lightly, carefully – with the palms of her hands to check that every strand of hair is still perfectly in place. Benjy and Mary are purring like tractors, wrapped around her legs. Their present's next: tins of Whiskas. Leaning floppily against the coat cupboard, I'm pleased to not be at school – to be soaking in her activities.

Leda leaps on to the table. She is offensively regal-stanced. Dad would hurl her, serve her right. That's one thing I can't understand – Mrs Taylor's liking for Leda. In most matters her loyalty's with us. But she can seem to forget how Leda came to be here. This does make me fidget, aggravated. But it won't help my turn for attention to come quicker.

I envy Benjy and Mary for openly, loudly miaowing their excitement and impatience, claw-jumping wildly as Mrs Taylor forks out the lumps of brown-jellied meat. Benjy's nearly choking, trying to purr and gobble at the same time.

And now, Mrs Taylor's smiling face is turned to me. I feel I must be glowing.

'Go on, then,' she tells me with a teasing flick of her finger towards the far corner of the dining-room, as if she doesn't know that I've been delaying for her approval.

Cocooned in my blanket, I trip and rush-shuffle

over.

It's illicit, the pleasure I'm about to get, because Dad thinks when I'm ill I spend the day in bed. I'd be in Mrs Taylor's way if I did. Upstairs, she has to Hoover, clean windows, rip sheets off for washing. Downstairs, there's a section she won't touch: all along the wall that is Dad's study area. So it is *under instruction* that I sit here, by the filing-cabinet in front of the window, in his swivel chair.

The sweetly disorienting smell of coffee being made is heaven. I move my finger to only millimetres from the sheep's skull Dad uses for a paperweight. With the flat of my hand I follow the horizon of his file-stacked, book-strewn desk that is solid beside me. And now Mrs Taylor is coming over. I am getting dizzy from pleasure. She's not starting on her cleaning routine straight away.

It's almost too fast for me to feel it, but her hands are whisking round me doing swift tuckings-ins. My skin is tingling.

I'd like it if she'd stop and chat. But I know she must give herself strict rules if she's to get everything done. She perches near me on the window-sill. It's a brief relaxation I'm grateful for, even if it's quickly that she sips her steaming drink. I wish I could know everything she's thinking.

My eyes dart, searching for what her mind is on. Damn that horseshoe behind the kitchen door, hanging upside down, as it always has. I don't know why. I very much want Mrs Taylor to turn it right way up, to stop the luck falling out instead of in.

If even Mrs Taylor won't, it's like our fate is sealed. I look to her for reassurance.

I find it merely in the way she's putting down her coffee-cup and rolling up the sleeves of her pale yellow hand-knit.

Mrs Taylor is blinkered like a horse once she starts work. She won't stop for lunch. I've never seen her eat anything except the corner of a biscuit. **43**

I can imagine there's a voice inside her head instructing that this and the other *must* be done, and they must be done according to a precise schedule, with any time left to be used for optional extras, such as sorting out that larder – dreadful! – rice next to jam next to wood glue. But first, get out the dustpan and brush . . .

The straightforward purposefulness of her can make me feel empty. But mostly, it lulls my mind, the sound of her speeding along her invisible path round the house.

That's except for . . . there is one other place Mrs Taylor won't touch. I won't go there either, or Max or Phyll, and definitely not Dad. The room off the kitchen, where *she* kept her stuff before she sent the removals men.

When the removals men started heaving her stuff out, Dad stayed working at his desk, brittle. Me and Max and Phyll retreated under the ivy that hangs down the wall outside by the stone trough. Threads of refusal to react linked even through the granite wall to Dad. None of us would say one word to the removals men.

The russet velvet armchair came out upside-down, its four brass wheels spinning on the ends of its legs, a neat cigarette burn in the arm, brocade trimming trailing down the path.

The sun was shining. Swallows were nesting in the big barn's eaves.

Boxes, crates, suitcases – it seemed that it was never going to end.

Me, Phyll and Max kept our shoulders touching under the ivy. The last thing out was the lamp: faded silk shade, crimson tassels unravelling, chipped base.

Afterwards, the room off the kitchen still had boxes and chair-legs and lamp bases marked out in the dust. It's a junk room now. We don't go in, except to pile up rubbish.

We never had to explain to Mrs Taylor.

She is on her way through to the living-room. Seeing her, I realise my face was painfully contorting. I twist it out to humble pleading. I grip my flimsy fingers on to the plastic arms of Dad's swivel chair.

Hoover attachments are balanced and weaved all about Mrs Taylor's shoulders, arms and neck, so probably she'll have to carry on through to the living-room.

But, no. She *does* stop. She fixes eye contact.

She says, 'You're hard on Max. He misses his mother.'

I am outraged. I want to say I'm extremely *tolerant* with Max, considering his constant whining. But she is already gone, engulfed in the rattling sounds of the Hoover.

I stare at the empty doorway.

I helped Max build his brick road the other day. I got his smart shirt ready for the school photographs. What about Max being good to *me* for a change?

It's not fair! Like last time I was 'ill', when I was talking to her about Phyll taking my pencils – I'd spent all evening sharpening them, but Phyll forced them from me on the way to school, so I was the one who got reprimanded for not having any. Mrs Taylor didn't sympathise. I waited for her to, but instead she told me: 'Phyll has decided for the moment that she has to look after herself, because she thinks no-one else will; she'll soften – be patient.'

That's all very well, but *what about my pencils*? And there's the way she pushes and thumps if things don't go her way. How come I have to watch out for Phyll and Max all the time?

Mrs Taylor marches flagrantly *past* me and outside.

I will get back at her. Pettily vengeful: I prepare a mortally hurt expression. She's returning into the house, washing bundled in her arms.

It seems no amount of me emanating the pain of a wounded defenceless animal will make her want to nurture me. She marches straight upstairs. I am mortified for real. I hear her strip the beds of their sheets for the first wash.

Why won't Mrs Taylor come out with something soothing? It is usual: one comment that's hard, one helpful.

She goes past. I glare down. I try to think myself healed with other things she's said. Like about how people say the way I use words makes me precocious, and I think, pre-co-cious, what's that? Then I look it up in the dictionary and want to use it. Mrs Taylor told me that it is something praiseworthy, and if people have insult in their voice, then it's because they feel threatened. So whenever anyone says I'm precocious, I think of Mrs Taylor and her words help.

But just remembering how she can be is not enough. The sounds of bristle, back forth back forth as she scrubs the table is abrasive to my ears. I wait. She turns the chairs on top of the table ready to wash the kitchen floor. I'm getting desperate for my pacifier. The mopping's finished. What if she has given up on me? She lays newspaper down to protect and dry the floor.

On her way upstairs with the Windowlene and a duster, surely now! I turn the chair to follow her movements.

She does her just-checking-the-patient's-all-right glance and suddenly – finally – stops. My heart leaps. Fear is too inbred. I furrow my eyebrows, like Dad does, warning.

She's almost sad when she says, 'Allie –' she never wastes words normally; obviously she's talking to me ' – you've had to grow up too fast.'

Full stop.

I clutch my body to the chair's seat and arms and back. I shuffle my brain to try and make some sense.

Other people say things like that: 'You're too adult for your age.' Children are supposed to play games, which I do, and fight their brothers and sisters, which I do. Adults smoke cigarettes and drink whisky; I go to school. People say I understand too much, but I have problems with arithmetic in class – just like other children.

What do they mean?

Rashly, I *demand* of Mrs Taylor, 'Explain!'

But Mrs Taylor has closed her expression from me. She purses her lips and narrows her eyes then *snaps*, that I've moved too far out; she needs to wash this bit of floor; I must get out of her way. My heart might burst. She says more softly maybe she'll explain another time. She tries to tweak my ear playfully.

I've had two hard and only one helpful comment from her. I want to rip every hair off my head and gouge my eyes. I pull away from Mrs Taylor.

Dad's car crunches gravel into the yard. I kick at his chair despairingly. I know he's back from work with only seconds to spare to fetch Mrs Taylor down to the bus-stop in time.

Dad's entire being, standing impatient in the doorway, is oblivious to me. *I'm out of bounds*, I want to tell him, *can't you see? You should be reprimanding*.

His voice is directed at the ceiling. He's charging upstairs to fetch her.

I *refuse* to see Mrs Taylor swift-marching past. I hear her *stupid* voice going on to Dad some boring rubbish about how she's just got to that stage with a favourite skirt when she realised it's better to invest in a new one than carry on stitching up the old seams.

Why does Dad want to know that? He's got to rush her for the bus. GET OUT!

The back door echo-shuts like I'm in a cell.

I trail my blanket, up to where she was sorting and folding in the corner of Dad's room. She must despise me. I look madly around, grasping for something that will tell me in reality she cares.

The ironing-board's not clear as usual. My eagerness ridicules itself. I missile to the other side of the room Max's brown corduroys – that are third hand through me and Phyll and were cast-offs even before that. How can the shabbiness of these examples of our school clothes show she cares?

■

This buying trip is all down to Mrs Taylor. It is exciting and confusing. I'm like a rabbit caught in headlights, only it's the fluorescent glare of a vast store's lights. Dad, towering in shadow, holds up two pairs of thick green cotton knickers.

'Which size?' his booming voice demands.

Phyll's twirling a strand of hair around her finger like she's not even trying. I scrutinise each item in turn. And again.

I don't know. I feel despair. The two knickers look the same. Too big? Too small? No amount of effort helps me reach a conclusion.

Dad looks stumped. Then, 'Get a basket,' he declares with new determination.

'Right,' Dad says and suddenly we're having to follow fast behind – me, Phyll, Max – mixing up walking and running steps in order to keep up.

Dad is storming down the aisle, grabbing things from left and right and tossing them into the basket. Mothers and grandmothers are careering to keep out of his way. Dad's oblivious to everything except what he's decided to do.

48   My eyes are going mad, following his hand

movements. Trousers – he picks out three different sizes. Shirts, skirts, pullovers – three different sizes.

I think I see his plan. He's picked out a variety of sizes of every item he thinks we'll need. And now, clothes trailing out of his overloaded basket, he is looking for . . .

An assistant. We trot behind. He veers in front of the targeted nylon-tunic woman.

'Ah!' he says to this staff member. 'Would you mind very much,' he says with a grave expression on his face, 'giving me your advice?'

My face swings swiftly from him to her, dutifully concentrating.

The woman says she would be glad to be of service.

Dad explains that his three children need clothes – I suppress glee that he's paying all this attention to us – and he points to his basket, presumably to illustrate that although he doesn't have the knowledge necessary to make the final choice he has at least made a good start.

My ears try to sift through to the essentials of what the assistant is gushing: she understands his problem; there are no changing rooms; it is hard to judge a child's size simply by looking . . .

At agonisingly long last she comes to her summation: for precisely all these reasons each item is labelled not only according to size but also according to age.

I am so excited I can't stop myself. I grab a shirt that has a nine year old's label sticking out and hold it up against myself. I must be extremely skinny. It will be massive on me. But it has no holes or patches.

■

On Saturday we were buying clothes. On Sunday we are being told to clean the house.

I don't understand.

Dad has changed. He is not allowing me to stand behind him over by the cooker, ready to support him.

I had become familiar with how he can be distant or raging or unpredictable, with not knowing and needing to find out. It gave me a role that could, it's true, be unnerving. But it made me crucially important. Standing here, I am nothing. He has ordered me into line, with the *others*, in front, facing him. He does not even address me first.

'Max. Hoover.' His voice is commanding dismissive. I snap my legs rigid-straight, resisting in advance.

I am rebelliously pleased that Max is making such a clattering mess of getting out the Hoover. He's bound to break the stretchy pipe, the way he's wrapped it round his waist to drag the rest along the floor.

Dad will soon see he can't just carry out these plans without consulting me.

'Phyll. Rubbish,'

I fold my arms. This will certainly be disastrous. Phyll only sucks her thumb and fingers harder. She's one-handedly trying to get the bin-bag out. Tins and packets and teabags are tumbling on to the floor. Dad will regret this.

'Allie. Washing.'

I have accepted much worse things than orders, like getting yelled at from exploded temper for things that weren't my fault.

I will make Dad repeat himself. I squash my feet inside my T-bar shoes until they are intransigent. I will not move.

Dad's picking up the broom. That's undermining. I didn't realise he was planning to join in too.

'Don't just stand there,' he says to me, not even cross; more enthusiastic to get going. 'Get a move on.'

I happily accepted the regimentation of Dad's solution to the question of regular exercise – the Sunday morning swim. Because even his brusque commanding can't obliterate my luxuriously overwhelming feeling that we're on a family outing.

And then, once I am in the pool, there is the rare sensation that I would like to have forever, that I am in my element.

I can be spontaneous in my crawl/breast-stroke cross-breed, kicking like a frog or splashing, whatever feels right, of my body's own accord. Like last week I suddenly found I was gaining adrenalin-momentum by tossing my head from side to side, far over, so my ears hit the water. Then I sank down under and wiggled my feet like flippers. Other people's half-bodies were distorted, massive – tiny – wobbly, and I could weave in between them, without them seeing. I didn't even mind that the chlorine made my eyes bright red itchy afterwards.

But today I am loathing everything. It is like Dad has found out my secret pleasure is to be completely, thoroughly, *in* the water. Otherwise, why would he be now making us stand on the edge?

'To learn to *dive*,' he says. It is just a bullying exercise of his control. 'Could save your lives one day,' he said. Like when?

I can feel Max and Phyll on either side of me emanating resentment too. My goose-bumps are assisting, swelling more distinct, tingeing bluer. Water laps over the tiled edge, over my feet. But with this new threat of being forced to dive, I am hating its caress. It is with aggression that I watch an old man do a dive at the deep end of the pool. It is like he is an enemy collaborator, making it look easy. Up, over, splosh.

Standing teeth-chattering here, so high up from the sparkling surface, it seems it would be a plain ridiculous thing to do, to hurl myself forward and flip **51** my legs over my head. I'd either drown or crack my head on the side, I'm sure. And why dive when I could climb down the steps, which is after all what they're for?

'I can't do it,' Max says. I press my elbow into his arm, to indicate I am in full support of how he's getting into his whine. 'Dad, I can't!' he grates louder.

I sneak a glance round to see how Dad's reacting. He looks furious-impatient. We should be allowed at least to voice our objections.

Suddenly he's barking, 'All right, I'll dive.'

This is a surprise. But I get my jaw quick back up from dropping, because it is an entirely welcome one. I don't know why I didn't think of it before. It was his daft idea. He should do it first.

I scrutinise him. He didn't feel he had to show us how to wash-up or cook. *Learn by your mistakes* is how he got round those ones.

'Here, hold my glasses,' he says to Max.

If I didn't know better, I'd think it was fear twinging his eyebrows out of place.

'Don't drop them,' Dad tells to Max.

This is not necessary. Max wouldn't risk even tinily loosening his grip on Dad's glasses. I have an odd suspicion that he's stalling.

He's concentrating hard on the man at the other end of the pool, who must be a dim blur with Dad's eyesight. It seems Dad's intent on what the blur's doing, so he can do the same. In fact, it's nothing like. Dad lifts his arms above his head and stretches his hands into the air. They're much too far forward and his back is hunched.

Now I am definite, his hands are shaking.

He shuffles till his toes are just over the edge, clutching like a gorilla. He bends his knees. He pauses. He takes a deep breath. Another pause. Deeper

I am goggle-eyed. The world could be coming to an end and I wouldn't notice. Dad is nervous. And he has not stopped us seeing.

He hurls himself into the water. Bham! That has to be the worst and loudest belly-flop ever. He has never dived before in his life. That's clear now. He is completely exposed – to pain and ridicule. Not from us, of course, but I daren't look round in case any other swimmers are laughing.

He catapults out of the water. His chest is bright, luminous red. He's spluttering and reeling.

I am horrified.

'My glasses,' he says coughing, spraying chlorinated water from his lungs.

He can see us now, so we have to flatten our expressions. Completely seriously, he says, 'That's how you do it. Now it's your turn.'

You have to be joking! No *way* am I doing that. He did it, so we've got to . . .

The old man has come round. I'd like to drown him. He's offering to teach us how to dive.

'Thank you,' Dad says. 'You're extremely kind,' his voice wobbly like I thought only mine went when I'm trying not to cry.

Dad is not allowed to do that. It makes me feel he has chopped away every bit of my stability. I make sure he is out of my sight, where he's gone to sit near a window.

I turn my flurried attention to the old man.

He wants us diving off the side within half an hour and off a board by next week. To avoid my eyes wandering to Dad, I will be minutely obedient.

This man has a technique: build up to the dive gradually. Start off in the water, on a step, so that it's not so much a dive as a lunge forward. Then do this lunge off the next step, then the next, until it turns nearly into a dive.

The slooshing of the water over my head is more promising of intense thrill than I could have imagined.

He has us crouching on the side.

Do what you did on the steps, he says. Bend forward into the water, he says.

Now straighten up a bit: splosh.

That's it! I can dive!

I feel like I'm a dog's tail that's wagging so much I'm nearly falling over as I water-spray my way to where Dad is. I'm far ahead of Max and Phyll's running. 'Dad, Dad, did you see? I did it! I dived!'

I don't even listen for his, 'Very good.' I want his congratulation to be so thorough I can see it in his eyes. They're hardly even focusing. Phyll and Max are jostling. I shove them away. The man calls out that he hasn't finished with us yet. Max and Phyll are rushing back. First, I bite my lip, I take a panic breath, and I swift-touch Dad's shoulder in a direction that indicates I want them to be upright. He *will not* sit there hunched and helpless, chest still red, pained.

Now Dad will watch me!

'Watch us, watch us, d'you promise?' I've made him grunt acknowledgement. I practically soar back to the pool edge.

'Now, over my hand,' says the man. I pretend his hand's a wall and jump: up, over, splosh.

I can dive!

■

I have everything in hand.

Here on my walk out in the fields, the land is blanketed in white. The trees and walls and stones and every blade of grass have been subdued and made the same. Soft snowflakes fluttering and falling through the night have become in daylight crystalline all over to the skyline.

I breathe out great clouds of breath. I feel as powerful as if I am an ice queen. I stamp my feet, break through the micro-thin crisp surface to snow that crunches round my boots.

I did it right.

Max was distressed, of course, but he'll be grateful later.

It was as if the postman knew, making sure the brown paper parcel was delivered direct into my hands. Upstairs in mine and Phyll's room, hunched down between the beds, I explained to them the implications.

'It is a bad situation. We have been sent these without Dad knowing,' I said.

I understood how Max just wanted to rip open the Father Christmas paper that was tied with silver ribbons and bows. I kept a hand firm on his chest, forcing him to keep his distance.

'Think about it rationally,' I continued, glad that Phyll was only glowering and not trying to grab the presents from me. 'The objects would upset Dad. How could we enjoy them?'

''S not an *object*,' Max yelled. ''S my Christmas present from *my mummy*.'

Phyll and I became united. This was something we had to sort out between ourselves. Max was not allowed to shout for Dad's attention. Phyll quieted him.

'What's the point of presents if they have to be hidden in the barn?' I asked, intentionally rhetorical so it didn't matter that the gagging bedcover stopped him answering.

'It is the honest, upright thing to do,' I told his streaming, purple face. 'We must write a note on the package for the postman, "TAKE BACK TO SENDER".'

Here outside, in the freezing air that makes my breath come short and fast, I feel triumphant.

It is so simple. She is eliminated from my mind.

Today it is French.

Even Karen Crawley can't upset me. And especially not Miss Spinkster.

'Children! Children! Settle down!' Miss Spinkster claps her hands for attention.

It'll be *chou-fleur*, French for cauliflower, again – acting as if we're in a practical situation.

'Now,' she says. 'Into pairs.' She looks round, alarmed. We all know why. Unless the numbers are odd, she can't play. 'Julie dear,' she say, 'you must be tired. Perhaps you'd like to go outside and rest, or something?'

Julie doesn't look tired. She looks bored. She wasn't even faking weakness. She was drumming her fingers, waiting for Miss Spinkster to let her go, impatient.

On the way out Julie steals a half pint of milk. She will pour it down the drain.

I am so concentrating on Julie Reed my mind is drifting dangerously as I turn my chair. I'm facing Karen Crawley. I should have known she'd make sure to sneak round.

'You're my partner,' she says. I try to make my expression look like irritation. Karen will taunt me about my clothes. I remind myself I am prepared.

She scrapes her chair towards me menacingly. Trust her to have a bigger, *red* bobble chair. On my short legged yellow bobble chair, I crane my neck. Karen still towers over me. She's going to try and make me fluff my lines. But I've been watching Julie Reed. I hope I've learned her tricks.

It is the same routine as usual written on the blackboard.

Customer: '*Un chou-fleur, s'il vous plaît.*'

Shopkeeper: '*Un chou-fleur?*'

Customer: '*Oui.*'
Shopkeeper: '*Voilà, un chou-fleur.*'
Customer: '*Merci.*'

Karen says, 'You're t'customer. I'm t'shopkeeper.'

I don't care which role I play.

I ask for a cauliflower. '*Un chou-fleur, s'il vous plaît.*'

Karen shrieks her line. The volume is for Miss Spinkster's benefit. After quickly glancing round, Karen thrusts her piggy face forwards. 'Scruffy – scruffy – scruffy,' she hisses.

'Jus' look at yer,' she snorts disgustedly. 'My mum ses she'd 'ave left too. Scruffy – scruff-ffy.'

I don't even let myself get disorientedly upset by the sick feeling, because she can't see it, I think.

I speak my part: '*Oui.*' Karen continues to hiss. I'd like to say it doesn't suit her. Pigs don't hiss. But instead I say her part: '*Voilà. Un chou-fle—*'

She butts in angrily, 'Yer can't do that! Tha' wa' mine!'

I say, '*Bien.*' I learnt the word from a book. Miss Spinkster hasn't taught it so Karen doesn't know it.

'Wha' du' tha' mean?' Her snorting turned up nose is going purple. 'You can't purr i' in. Yer cheatin'.'

'*Bien,*' I say.

'Mi-isss,' she calls out. She thinks she will force me to play her way. Miss Spinkster approaches. I am on my own game.

I start by quivering my chin. This moves my lip. Next I quiver my nostrils. A quivering chin isn't necessarily convincing, but quivering nostrils – a brilliant, authentic touch.

Miss Spinkster has fallen for it even faster than I could have hoped. She gabbles that I'd better go and do the felt appliqué, that is: remove myself – and more especially the possibility of tears – to the empty far side of the classroom.

I *have* learnt from Julie using the hole in her heart, how to turn a handicap into a weapon.

Karen seethes.

I am heady with success. I reel over to where the felt appliqué is laid out on three tables pushed together.

It is undermining that Paul Cragg gave me that look, his blue eyes wide and questioning, like he's asking me if this really is a right course of action.

My eyes go defensively away from him, searching out of the window. There's Julie Reed, over by the school gate, destroying dandelions. She is staring after a tractor that is rattling down towards the main road.

Is this listlessness I can see?

She bullies, she steals, she lies – all because she can get away with it. I thought I'd understood.

Julie Reed's bit on the felt appliqué is a fence. It's not a pretty fence. She didn't sew on strips of soft brown felt. She found black twigs and glued them round the village school.

And then suddenly I realise. There is a fundamental flaw in her plan. Here the class is small enough and Miss Spinkster weak enough. She can dominate. But the same tricks are not transportable when it is time to go to Big School.

If Julie's tricks won't work at Big School, then nor will mine.

The pupils who are leaving all got given presents by Miss Spinkster.

I didn't even feel pity for her, despite the way she stood by her desk grasping a sodden lace handkerchief, her eyes red and swollen. We didn't like her. And her leaving presents were stupid: Bibles. She should know I'm not religious.

Ollie Ogden is tearing the pages of his to bits. With

a good soaking of spittle, they make pellets that even I am impressed by. He can get them to go a long way.

It's our last time coming back on this school bus from Skipwith. He is executing his parting revenge on Julie Reed.

I knew something like this would happen. I watch like a tragedy I know the outcome of.

Ollie settles a pellet of paper in the palm of his hand. He lines up his eye and: flick. Right at the top of Julie Reed's scar. He laughs, 'Ha, ha, ha!' sneering.

He is a despicable coward.

Karen Crawley comes round from the seat in front of Ollie Ogden, to join in. Ollie tells her to 'gerr away', then retracts almost immediately. They are united in their desire to get Julie Reed. We are leaving the school and her behind.

Splat! splat! splat! Ollie Ogden and Karen Crawley duck back down behind the seat, their hands over their mouths, their bodies contorted with sniggering.

I sink in my centre-of-the-bus seat. I am impotent.

I stare wistfully at Paul Cragg untangling a knot of fishing wire. Then I wonder, why's he not doing anything?

Splat! One of the pellets strays by a few inches and hits him in the face. He jerks his head up, surprised, then he looks at Julie.

She is stiff as a doll, staring straight in front of her. I think she knew all this would happen; that it has not finished yet.

Julie Reed ruled for a long time. The rebels will need to see her suffer if they are to have their satisfaction.

Paul makes do with warning Ollie Ogden and Karen Crawley that he cleaned his airgun last night. They lean over and tease Dawn Crawley, 'Fat and ugly! No-one'll want t'marry you – fat and ugly!'

Will Reed is waiting for the school bus at the

telephone box as usual. When he sees it cranking up the hill he runs with excitement, lifting his jumper.

'Mong!' Ollie Ogden shouts out of one of the top sliding windows. William runs round the Pillar, tugging at his jumper. Ollie Ogden glares at Julie with undisguised hostility, challenging.

He elbows to get off the bus first. He runs over to Will Reed and pushes him, hard, glaring back at Julie who is coming down the steps.

Ollie Ogden pushes again, harder. Will falls backwards and hits the ground. Will is screaming now.

Then suddenly Ollie Ogden is being hammered. Julie is hammering with her fists, relentlessly, furiously.

Karen Crawley falls silent. The Pickering boys shuffle. Julie doesn't stop.

Ollie Ogden cowers, shields himself with his arms. He whimpers. He crawls, runs out of her reach.

Julie is crimson. She is clutching her chest. Real, sharp pain. She has to drag the air into her, grating. When her voice comes out it is broken. 'Leave-'im-be.' Barely audible.

William's eyes are full of terror. Still on the ground, he feels for her hand.

To the side of me and Max and Phyll, the group is huddled. It is silent, bewildered.

The Julie Reed I revered has been defeated.

Dad's gone on to a new level of coping. His dinners are revolting in a way that would be touching – for the effort – if it wasn't for the fact that they make me retch.

His latest thing is yeast tablets, bought in bulk from the chemist. Today Max has decided to reduce his two yeast tablets to powder. This is an entertaining distraction for me. He has wrapped them in paper towel. He has got out the meat tenderiser. I relish the chaos of the way Max's pulverising is catapulting plates and glasses into the air. Dad's rules are so clearly defined now, we understand exactly when to stop. Split seconds before Dad's mouth opens to shout 'Enough!' Max has dropped the tenderiser.

He has success! The yeast tablets are reduced to a fine powder. Elbows discreet on the table, I pop my face on my hands. Max doesn't know yet that the dinner is more revolting than the yeast tablets. Bean stew.

Dad calls it cassoulet. He says it's economical, fibrous, nutritious – a brilliant way of using up cheap cuts of pork.

The beans become cholesterol capsules. Phyll has surreptitiously spat her mouthful back on the fork and she's sucking her thumb and fingers quietly.

'Dad! Dad! I can't swallow the fat!' Max says. I don't know what other part of the stew he thinks he's going to eat. But if he can play it right we might all get let off. 'It's making me sick!' he says.

I try to show willing by having a go on the sea-kale. Sea-kale is actually cow-feed. I told Dad this, but Dad said no.

Dad thinks he has control. I have my methods.

I stuff the leaf in whole, chew like mad to get it as mashed as possible, and then swallow hard. I know Max will try to copy me. He always gags on sea-kale.

And, here he goes, right on cue, charging over to the sink shouting, 'Dad! Dad! I can't,' sticking his fingers down his throat and pulling out a long rope of semi-masticated sea-kale stalk. More and more keeps coming out, like handkerchiefs unravelling from a magician's hat, only white-putrid-looking.

Dad will now relax his eat-everything-on-the-plate rule. Covertly of course.

He leaves the room for long enough for us to dash to the swing-bin and scrape our food in.   **61**

When he comes back globs of bean stew are spilled all down the side of the swing-bin, clearly visible. He turns a blind eye. We're back safe in our seats, angelic.

'Finished!' we cry in unison, eyes wide open, hands neat in our laps.

'OK, well done,' Dad says. 'You can get down then – but don't forget the washing-up!' he adds.

We wait till he's picked up his whisky and his cigarettes and gone to the living-room. Then we quarrel. About who's turn it is to wash.

In fact, it's not a quarrel. Phyll and I decide it's Max's turn. He protests. Why? He washed-up last night! Phyll and I do our double act: I talk; she towers. Assaulted by my words and Phyll's physical presence, Max doesn't stand a chance. But he has his pride! This is *not* a defeat. He insists that he wanted to wash anyway. He wouldn't do the drying if we paid him.

I'm thinking maybe I should talk Dad into buying disposable. If I just happen to mention the merits of paper plates, paper cups and so on, he might take the hint. Or he might not.

Really I want him to go back to the kind of cooking he did before he got experimental: Fray Bentos steak pies in handy throw-away tin trays; German ring sausages cooked in disposable plastic packages. They were perfect. But bean-stew pans are a nightmare. It's a good job Max is doing the washing-up.

■

Everything was going so well. We all four of us felt really strong.

Sat now on the cold stone bench, images are battering me. I try to rap sense into my head with my knuckles. They make no imprint. I hammer harder.

62   It was just a cat that died.

It was Mary; she was with us through the move out here, through our mother leaving – she'd had her kittens on my bed.

Dad says she had a good life. I cannot see how that makes it in any way all right.

I shake my skull till inside it's thunder and lightning.

How can a cat compare with what else is happening? But I am ripped apart by the fact that it was Dad who suggested giving her a proper burial, for the sake of me and Phyll and Max. He is an atheist. He has no love for animals. He dug the hole in the far corner of the back field.

It took one shovelful of earth to fill her in.

Why?

Why us?

Mary died. That was enough pain. Then there was the burglary.

I tell myself, be rational. I have thought of this too much already. They are only material possessions. It's like I have been violated.

I press my legs on to the cold stone bench, as if with enough will-power I can become as feelingless.

I didn't know what to do.

Dad not home; Phyll and Max mad-eyed, waiting for me to make it like it'd never happened.

Dad's books! Why did they have to decimate his books? They should have been able to see it was a crappy hi-fi before bothering to yank the wires that ran along inside the bookcase to the speakers.

I know that the component parts are only ink, paper, binding-cloth and glue. Seeing his books sprayed out on the floor – crushed pages, broken spines – I felt like screaming my voice-box to shrapnel. They were the most precious things he owned.

I can understand the wedding rings. Perhaps it could be a relief for Dad they took them. It clearly **63** wasn't a proper storing place, in his sock drawer. It was almost soothing for me, the physical activity of picking the two empty jewellery click cases from out of tumbled, threadbare socks.

I stuffed the rings' containers safe to the bottom of the bin. But I couldn't be clear-sighted with the photographs.

I don't know what they thought they'd find up there, swiping everything off the top shelf of his walk-in cupboard. The briefcase full of photos from when we were little was spurted on the floor.

I just stood there. My mind absorbed itself in referencing. Snap-shot of a couple: Mum and Dad – turtle-necks, black ski-pants, arms entwined, ecstatic smiles. Curling black-and-white of me, Phyll and Max on a Mexican rug, me and Phyll not dressed, holding tiny, swaddled Max, surprised. Later, Mum alone against the fireplace – hating.

Something deep inside said, *Allie, laugh at these flat records of how your life is failing. Laugh.* Instead, I found that I was crying. Through distorting, stinging liquid I stared hysterical, grabbing, shoving back in the briefcase.

Dad seemed OK about the burglary. He raged and blasphemed about his books, of course. But I'd got every photograph cleared away in time before he got home.

The stone bench gets the evening sun, but it is cold.

It was just before supper, everything was cleared and Dad had made at least two almost jolly comments. I wanted the burglary to disappear quickly to the past. Chirruping falsely, I dashed from Dad to Max, to Phyll, to Dad – group cheering.

I decided I had to talk to Dad but I couldn't find him anywhere. I thought, 'I know – the vegetable patch!' I ran out into the garden, but I couldn't see him. Just rows of beans, peas and carrot tops; no Dad.

I don't know why I looked round the corner to the plum tree. I don't know why I did, because he shouldn't have been there, but he was. Under the branches.

I saw his hands were covering his face. I was so much wanting everything to be all right, I thought for a split second maybe he was preparing his eyelid trick, the one he used to do, when we were tiny infants, for fun?

I began to speak. 'Dad— ' and stopped short.

His hands came down. It was like his whole body was collapsing.

He'd have told us to stand up straight. He'd have stuck his index finger in the small of our backs so we'd squirm and go, 'Dad, don't *do* that!'

His head was hanging. His hands, big hands, are always active – cooking, writing, steering, slapping one of us for getting out of line. But they stayed hanging. His glasses had slipped down his nose. Right down, and he didn't push them up. His face was wet, open-pored, dripping – from his nose and mouth and chin. Swollen lids, bloodshot eyes. Streaming.

Wash your face, Dad, and pull yourself together! Splash cold water, go on!

It doesn't help us. It wouldn't help him.

I said again, 'Dad . . . ' He didn't move. Maybe he heard, maybe not. It's irrelevant. I was no use.

Slowly. Quietly. I walked backwards. Round by the side gate. Here.

I turn options over in my mind and reach the same conclusion. I can do nothing.

1975

I am reconstructed.

It is my first day at Big School. I am taller. Older. I am nearly ten miles away from home, in a *town*. But I'm not scared.

And for this reason it is extra annoying that Karen Crawley still feels she can hiss 'Scruffy!' in my ear then push past disdainfully. Apart from anything else, I'm *not* scruffy now. At least, not compared to how I used to be. That's the whole point.

Watching Karen Crawley walk ahead of me, I want to yell and run and smash her with my fists. But letting her get to me does not fit with my image. She is not significant.

It is 8.55 a.m. and I am standing just inside the wire mesh school gates. I draw breath right down to the bottom of my lungs.

Dizziness; head ready to swim up into the air. Vital seconds lost regaining balance. Deep breathing not a successful ploy.

I am reconstructed.

There were stages that had to be gone through. They took me months. First, there were these glasses – brown tortoiseshell with an extremely large number of dark swirls in them, so they actually do look black, except under close scrutiny. And nobody will be getting close enough to do that.

My new glasses are pleasantly heavy on the bridge of my nose. They distract all attention from the wishy-washy colour of my eyes. By everyone's standards, they are extremely ugly.

If the worst comment I get is 'speccy four eyes', I will be disappointed.

It is my first day at Big School. It is vital that the immediate impression I make is as I planned.

My fringe is grown long enough to touch nearly all along the top edge of my new glasses. It's like the fringe and plastic frame are joined together, a mask that can be slotted off and on for complete disguise when necessary.

Like now. There's all these children, of more shapes and sizes than I thought existed. They keep on barging past. And I fear that I've seen only a small percentage of the actual pupils.

I wriggle my neck inside the stranglingly tight collar and tie. I certainly got that right, my degree of prissiness. My navy and sky blue striped tie-knot is practically pea-sized. Most pupils haven't even got theirs on yet, or they're busy lassoing themselves with pre-knotted ones as they go.

The reconstruction is successful.

I have practised the necessary walk. I begin to do it up the drive.

No mincing stepping. Arms stiff at my navy V-neck jumpered side. Hurl each leg forward as if it has a ten-ton weight packed into the heel, making sure no-one notices that my white-socked calves look like squashed paper straws below knees so knobbly that when I do extra long strides they hook the hem of my A-line navy skirt.

The school's soot-blackened clock-watchtower comes into view over the drive's horizon.

Stride invincibly on.

I assess the rising section of main school building: black bricks stacked like lookout posts along the sharp roof; top-floor windows like reflecting eyes. There's so much building I can't take it all in at one glance.

Where's the sounds of 'Tig Off Ground' and 'What's the Time Mr Wolf?' And skipping games? And conkers?

The breaktime noises are crashing. As I walk, they get more deafening and threatening than if they were coming from industrial machinery.

There's not one but *three* wired-off playgrounds. The farthest away one is practically empty, with two sentries. I don't like the look of them one bit: hair spiked on top, long at the nape. The flapping hems of their voluminous bottle-green trousers incorporate not one but zillions of uniform-defying colours in the strips of garishly coloured tartan up the sides. And their shirts are made out of neither crisp cotton nor static-electric polyester but out of skin tight stretchy material. They do have collars, and here is the only clue that they're pupils: dashes of the school's navy and sky blue at the necks. These dashes are horizontal rectangle remains of ties knotted so loose that there is barely a centimetre of tongue left to hang down.

The tie seems to be a main clue to degrees of rebellion. The longer the tongue, the younger and more obedient the pupil, hence full six and seven inch tongues in the playground nearest the main school-building entrance.

My tie tongue is stretched to nine inches. I am prissily invincible, nearly. My positioning is crucial.

The raised section between the concrete pillars, **71**

directly below the staff-room is, I think, the best vantage point for several reasons.

1. Here, I can lean against the pillar and no-one can get behind me.
2. The proximity to teachers makes me an instantly dislikable swot candidate, and yet being perpendicular to the overhead window outcrop, no teacher can actually see me.
3. Most important: on this raised section, I have full view of all three playgrounds. When the bell rings for the start of school, they'll have full view of me. It will be immediately evident to the most influential pupils that I am not worth bothering with.

That's the theory. I am somewhat unsettled by the positioning of Karen Crawley.

Age-wise, she and I ought to be in the first playground.

Certainly, there's not much to recommend Playground One. Most of its children have their fingers clutched into the wire fence while they stare in awe at the older pupils. Karen's edging nearer the gate of Playground Two.

I have great dislike for Karen Crawley, but in a way this is quite courageous. Or foolishly naive.

The occupants of Playground Two do not look pleasant. A gang of boys periodically decide to climb as high as they can up the criss-crossing twangy metal fence, not to climb over but so they can practise *hurling* themselves down on to the tarmac and still stay able to get up and climb again.

And now two girls in the centre of Playground Two, poised aggressively, are beginning to circle each other. A boy at the top of the fence yells 'FIGHT!' He jumps down and hurls himself towards the action.

Almost instantly, the two girls are surrounded by an

enclosing circle of pupils. The word 'Fight' is repeated until it becomes a low ebbing chant.

'Fight–Fight–Fight– '

I ought to feel confident about this. Phyll and I fight. Or sometimes I fight Max. It involves a squabble and then some pushing and, if it's really bad, maybe a few quick whacking thumps until Dad comes and pulls us apart.

It's as if this fight is a leisure activity.

A very skinny girl, who really oughtn't be in Playground Two at all according to her height, has her tie-tongue at one-and-a-half inches. She seems too wheezy to do effective running. Is this some sort of initiation, the way she's hustling round the circle, collecting bits of people's jewellery. Against all my better judgement, I am nervous.

But I mustn't let anyone else see. Quickly I look around to check. Damn! I didn't spot Paul Cragg over there, away from the playgrounds, leaning relaxed against a tree – the only tree I can see, in fact: wiry, stubbornly continuing to grow, alone, by the drive side. It's not a *desirable* tree. It has no graffiti; there's still weedy sproutings at its base; no pupils' feet have worn the grass away to dirt. How come he doesn't feel he has to make an *effort*?

His uniform is confusing. All navy, yes, but not featuring a V-neck jumper. It's an army one like he always wore only not khaki green, and with his tie knot poking out the round neck. He's not stuck fishing-flies in the sleeve. That's something, I suppose. But he *is* making one of his stupid wire-loop rabbit traps. Those should have been left behind at *junior* school. How *dare* he feel so sure of himself that he can carry on making them here?

His fingers stop working briefly. His blue eyes look up at me from under his wild straw hair, and he is on the point of laughing, at *me*. I am *outraged*. But

I know that *he* is the fool. I concentrate on draining the blood from my face so that it is furious white under the pulled on glasses-hair mask. I will *not* let Paul Cragg distract me from my purpose.

Playground Two is what's important at the moment. Karen Crawley's just about to skulk inside the gate.

She had dressed with confidence that she would automatically be triumphant amongst her peers. She'd sliced not one but *two* enamel banana grips into her hair. She's had to slip them out surreptitiously. She's busy rolling her pristine white knee socks right down into her squeaky clean patent leather shoes, because none of the pupils wear *socks*. Even in Playground One, the girls have on adult nylon tights, in pretend-skin colour that's more like fudge shade.

I almost want to snigger that Karen Crawley got it so wrong, with her glaringly *pink* legs.

Inside Playground Two the fight is reaching fever pitch.

'Fight–Fight–Fight–' has blood lust in it now; the rotating circle of pupils is mimicking the foot pistoning and talon slashing that is going on inside. Some children shout out words of advice and encouragement. 'G'won! Dig 'er eyes out!'

At last, there is the sound of someone rapping, none too forcefully, on the glass above me. They do it again, slightly more emphatic this time.

The circle of pupils' faces spin and twist upwards, one split-second group glance checking out the gravity of the teacher-attention: clearly, this time action may be taken.

The circle disperses. Children sidle round the fencing. The two fighters do a couple more snarling get-*you*-laters at each other. It looks like neither has a scratch on her. They stalk, mutually victorious by default to opposite sides of the tarmac.

Karen Crawley sees her chance for group attention.

'Look,' she squeals, pointing a clenched trotter-hand in my direction. '*Speccy four eyes.*'

I almost feel embarrassed on her behalf. *That* won't impress anyone.

To my unpleasant surprise, I see that the dark-haired fighter is staring at me. All the hollowness of my stomach is filled up with burning molten liquids. I realise I am a convenient ploy for breaking away from the aborted fight situation with maximum dignity, minimum loss of face. It is not immediately clear, however, whether I will be the subject of the fighter's derision or protection.

I make a show of swinging my heavily be-spectacled head in an arc of bored resignation.

The fighter is setting off across the tarmac of Playground Two. I can't simply stand here. I have to do something to declare how I will respond to this ominous approach.

I stretch my head higher. I clasp my hands prissily in front of my A-line navy skirt. 'If she wants to waste her time bullying me,' my prim stance declares, 'then she can go right ahead. It's no skin off nose.'

Of course, if she decides to call my bluff it's a massive amount of skin off my nose, possibly quite literally. As I look at her clenched fist, I understand what the wheezy girl was collecting jewellery for. One swipe with these viciously spike-ringed fingers could remove half my face.

Why would anyone bother with a wimpish speccy four eyes? It'd hardly be a show of strength to bash *me* up.

But as the fighter's unmoving hair, skin-tight top and swirling skirt loom closer, I begin to wonder. The molten liquids in my stomach churn up into my chest. Following behind the fighter are a host of minions. **75**

Karen Crawley is trottering cautiously along the group's edge, preparing I presume to condemn or console me, whichever will get her most mileage. My breaths are getting distorted: they can't seem to go much further than the back of my throat, where they stick.

I thought I'd prepared for the worst. Backed against the concrete pillar, I am the focus of a semi-circle of comprehensive pupils who are edging hard-faced closer. All their tie-tongues are around two inches. I regret the defiance of tugging, as I came into school, my tie-tongue way below my skirt waist band.

The coal-haired fighter steps forwards and holds up her hand to stop the group's movement. I am trying very hard not to look, but I can see that she has blue eyeshadow and shimmering rust-colour streaked up her cheekbones. No *adult* I know wears so much make-up.

She inspects me. She takes her time about it. The churning goes into my head, but I know my nervously flickering gaze can be entirely hidden behind my glasses-hair mask – as long as I don't make eye contact. My neck kept rigid by my clamping collar, I aim my spectacles towards her bottle-green skirt. I decide this must make me look scared. I snap my head back up and swivel it, superfast, to see what else I can focus on.

Between two hair-spiked heads I see a hazy Paul Cragg leave his place by the tree and move nearer, in case I should need his assistance.

No *way* would I ever accept it, or, if I could help it, anyone else's for that matter. But I can use him as a foil. By glaring hostility at outsider Paul Cragg I can appear unaffected by the presence of this black-haired fighter. I figure this must help my status. I *glare*.

The fighter takes in my bitten fingernails and the safety-pin where I already lost a shirt cuff button, my absurdly thick heavy glasses and my straggly neither-here-nor-there colour hair.

She takes out a cigarette. My throat's twanging panic. Her pasty face lights up orange as she hunches over a match.

'Wha's yer Dad do, then, Four Eyes?' she demands curtly in an accent that's sourer than any in Skipwith or High Kirkby, and seems to need her to slice the corners of her mouth down. 'Well? Wha's 'e do?'

I'm unclear why she feels she must ascertain my father's occupation. I don't care what her Dad does. I conclude, however, that it is of no benefit to me to answer in any way other than straightforwardly. Although, I think a certain note of pomposity won't go amiss.

I raise my primly clasped hands and lecture for several seconds on the importance of my father's work in the field of *bibliography*, on the significance of his discovering dates when *Moving Type* began, on the value to *society* of him then *disseminating* this information.

I cut myself off abruptly to still appear in control when actually my breathing's having trouble getting even as far as the back of my throat. I glare up at the fighter.

Her glitteringly green-shadowed eyes narrow. 'Wha' yer tellin' us is tha' yer Dad's a *teacher*.' It looks like she might have to spit on me.

I nod defiantly, even though *everything* is churning now. The fighter takes a chest-inflating puff – right under the staff-room! I can't help feeling relief to see Paul Cragg step closer. The fighter turns away from me and begins to rabble-rouse her semi-circle of minions.

''S'e 'fraid ter gerr 'is 'ands dirty, or wha'?' she demands, jabbing a disdainful thumb over her shoulder in my direction.

Karen Crawley grunts a cautious, 'Yeah,' to indicate that that's just the way she thinks.

I reply to the bra lines of the fighter's tightly T-shirted back that, no, that's not the case at all.

77

The fighter is in her stride now, and I can see that I've had it. She rounds on me. I fiddle the bridge of my glasses about on my nose, wondering if I should take them off for safe-keeping before she hits me.

First, she wants more ammunition: 'Wha's yer mum do, then?'

Now *she's* had it. She'll look stupid when I tell her.

I explain haughtily that she doesn't even *live* with us.

This does stump the fighter. But it doesn't get rid of her. She's starting to get smilingly curious. She is staring at the flatness of my chest, as if there ought to be something there that isn't. Paul Cragg stops where he is while he waits to see what's going to happen. Karen Crawley puts a freeze on her expression to make it non-committal.

'So, yer's brought up by yer *Dad*, then?'

'I am indeed,' I snap, because if our mother doesn't live with us, then *of course* I'm brought up by my father.

The fighter leans forward, apparently with deep concern. Her breath is poison. She does a whisper that she can somehow aim more at the other pupils even though she's facing me. Her pencilled eyebrows quaver sympathy but her eyes glint hard.

''Ow are yer gonna ask yer *Dad* ferra *bra*?'

Now she's got me. It should be simple: don't need one, don't want one – no problem. But I'm not sure of my ground anymore. There's a pause when no-one else knows how her comment is meant either.

The fighter draws up to her full height and spits a venom laugh down at me. At least now I know how she meant it.

The semi-circled minions open their mouths to laugh derision at me. 'FLAT-CHESTED GEEK,' one declares

in a tone that implies the beginning of a group chant.

But suddenly the fighter changes her mind. With an elaborate patronising 'Awww', she whacks her arm around my shoulders and tweeks my cheek painfully.

I helped her get gracefully out of the aborted fight situation. She can afford to be magnanimous.

This changes everything. Mouths that had opened to deride clamp shut and force unwillingly into smiles.

Karen Crawley trot-sidles over to me. Smugness balloons her shiny pink cheeks. She has more claim on me, the leader's pet, than anyone else in the semi-circle, because I live in *her* village. *She* will patronise me too. Paul Cragg returns quietly to his place by the lone tree.

An electric bell announcing the start of my first day at Big School rattles my skull into numbness.

It has been a long day. I am ready to sleep. But I must pin my eyes open for a little while longer.

I leave the main bedroom light off and direct the pool of anglepoise light into the centre of my desk, with only centimetres to spare around today's page, so that I am eliminated, so that I concentrate entirely on the paper.

My new orange fine-ruled exercise book has nothing written on the front. It has no divisions of days, dates or anything, which is perfect. I will work things out quickly. Then I can tear those pages out and use the book for something else.

I want to do this fast.

I write very small in a handwriting that I have practised. It is plain. There are no give-away flourishes that tell if I'm adult or child, male or female.

I will organise my thoughts into numbered points between the lines. They will come together in a conclusion.

Monday. 9 p.m.
Progress with how I am perceived.

Only one day at big school, and it did turn out better than I could have hoped. The hair-glasses mask hid all evidence of my emotion so effectively that I feel sure it will enable me to actually not have the emotions before long. A lot of today wasn't by any means planned, but I realise it is completely perfect for Karen Crawley to be my friend. We have no liking for each other. It can be a relationship of mutual convenience.

Progress with how I am perceived is, without a doubt: '*Good.*'

■

Phyll is in awe of me. Her voice, calling my name from over by Dad's desk, is reedy and pathetic, *needing* me. Perhaps I will oblige. Just to show her how I don't give a damn.

She can never bully pens and pencils out of me again, because I am at *Big* School.

It's like a sadist game of hide-and-seek, the way I am pressed flat against the kitchen wall here – round the corner, out of her sight. I adjust the blue-stripe uniform tie at my throat with an impatient, practised thumb and finger twitch, as I've seen Dad do. I feel approximately twenty-five years Phyll's senior. I wait for her to call my name out for a third time.

'All-ie . . .'

She sounds the size of something like an ant, that I could squash without even thinking. I do an extra loud tongue 'tt' and a savagely bored huffing of my breath.

'All right,' I say, the most tired-of-this person in the world. 'I'm coming.'

I turn the corner, and find that it's not just Phyll standing lonely on the stone-tiled floor, but beside her **80** Max as well. What would she go to Max for before me?

And she usually takes such special care to be glowering in company.

But they cannot be friendly and think I'll care.

I maintain the patronising boredom, to them both.

'Well?'

Phyll has something in her hand. She holds it up: white and square with black squiggly, unknown writing on.

'So? You can read. Tell me what it says.'

'Explain it,' Phyll insists in a voice so small I understand her instruction more from the thrust out gesture of her uncertain hand.

Max is squinting up at me, warily expectant.

A haze that wobbles both their faces dissociates themselves from all responsibility.

Maybe I don't want it either!

Curiosity and apprehension are tangling my focus.

'I found it in Dad's desk drawer,' a blurry Phyll informs me surreptitiously.

Dad's drawer? This is not correct! I am clear again. Phyll has no right to go delving round in people's private things. I am coming to be furious. If I ever find she has been in *my* drawers, I will kill her.

'Go on,' she whispers loud, getting impatient.

I will get her for swapping allegiance by confiding in Max.

'This is from Dad's drawer!' I challenge severely, tapping the air with the white paper evidence as if it is a judge's hammer.

She looks at me in a way that says she can't believe the nonsense I can come out with. Her hands go on her hips; her lip curls into sneering. 'I can put it back where I found it,' she reminds me, like she's speaking to an idiot.

Suddenly I want her to be *my* friend. But more, I want the upper hand again. I give her a just-make-sure-you-do **81** look down my flaring nostrils. I grasp the piece of paper firmly between the fingertips of both my hands and give it a lightning, crease-removing thwack.

Phyll and Max jump. They glance around them. I can practically see their hearts thumping out of their chests. Ha!

They close in around me. I begin to read. It comes out explosion volume: *'For my darling Martin . . . '*

Shock makes my head jerk. He is Dad; Mr Bennett to everyone else. It is like I have had a piece of me wrenched away. Who dares to think they have the right to call him 'darling'?

I grip my glasses harder to my face. I must take control of the reverberating silence.

I skim the letter to myself.

But it's not a letter. I see from the shape it is a poem. Lines stand out, taking my attention.

The burning heat inside me.

It makes no sense! I keep my reading eyes impervious and knowing through their mask.

Who has the impudence to write such stupidness of 'body weeping' and a word I can't understand that must be 'organism' misspelt? For Max and Phyll, I shake my head to indicate: it's really not well written.

My body cries out.

The ending is a scrawl: *You have my – poison? pissing? passion?* Then some name that starts with *G*.

I am confused. Unexpectedly I feel like crying. What did I do wrong? I'd like Phyll to tell me not to worry and Max to stroke my hand. But they came crawling to me. I have to keep up this advantage. It is too tenuous. I can't let on.

'It seems to me,' I mumble, crooking my finger to my chin as if gripped by logic thought, 'hmmm . . . '

My mind is leaping randomly over years. It gets stuck, I'm not clear why, on the night I stumbled to the toilet and caught sight of a fair-haired woman who Dad

82

called a 'colleague' when I know she had nothing to do with his work in bibliography. She was naked, going across the hall towards the bathroom. I suppose she thought I hadn't seen her. She was, Dad'd said with too much emphasis and looking guilty, staying in the guest room.

I make sure I'm holding the piece of paper with dismissive certainty. I will not avoid their waiting stares. I glance at each with what I hope is something like contempt.

'It's from that colleague,' I announce wearily. 'It's not important.'

Even this land betrays me.

I am drained from panic; my legs are still madly running. They might turn to nothing and I would drag myself.

I could never get to far enough away.

Turbulent black sky has solidified. It is pressing down, choking the air. Angry light cuts under, slicing over bracken fronds. It presents this mass of stone before me as if it's something that is definite, reliable, here for centuries past and far into the future. I hurl myself towards it. The rock is loudly cold and sort of square and too big for me to wrap my arms around. It ought to make me feel secure. It started off as grains of sand.

Why has Dad turned to someone else, with secrecy and lying? I try my best.

Nothing is certain any more.

To my left is wire-mat grass. To my right is marsh that could drag a grown man down, right down and cover over. What if Dad leaves too?

Only hints of smirking wetness give the marsh away. The rest is non-committal tufts of dying green.

My head is ready to explode. I wrap my arms

around and around and squash until the pain is numbness.

■

My hair-glasses mask is securely in place.

A whole four weeks and a bit I've been at big school now. A total of twenty and a half days, and it feels like forever.

I can't imagine not being 'friends' with Karen Crawley.

Thank goodness she's not in my classes with me, so there is time I can keep for myself. Like now.

I make sure to sit on my own. Everyone else is clamouring to the back of the classroom. I make my T-bar Clarke shoes ring out in isolation on the puce-flecked lino, going forwards. This place, very near the blackboard, is exactly right.

On the razor-blade graffitied formica table-top, where it says *Bev 4 Gazzer 2 gether 4 ever 2 stay*, I clatter down my pens and pencils, a fanning artillery range in front of me.

If I keep my chairback tight up against the table behind, and do my snootiest head tilt, the inside seat next to me stays empty. No-one wants to be so prissily close to the teacher as I am.

I listen to the class behind me filling up. A rasping voice bludgeons into my space.

''Ere, shove over.'

I resist the command of this invader, who is hovering impatiently. I close my ears. I stare straight in front at pockmarks of dust plaster where gas-yellow gloss paint has been chipped away. The class noise protects me. I am implacable.

'G'won then!'

The sharpest elbow in the world is shoved in my
ribs.

I don't move for bullies, that's for definite. I skewer my glasses hard into the bridge of my nose, get in place my angriest jaw set and swivel-turn my head.

My glare is confused by popping-out eyes and cracked purple lips. It's the weed who was gathering the rings on the first day's playground fight.

'Yer gonner shove o'er, or what?'

The door is creeping open. The teacher Mr Beezley is coming in, his shoulders dragging. I can't risk that he might challenge me for keeping one place empty. I scramble and scrape chair-legs to let the skinny weed sit down.

With someone directly next to me I'm not so sure of myself.

'Took yer time,' she rasp-whispers, 'didn't yers?'

Is she angry? No. She winks a veiny eyelid. Her lips look too dry for smiling.

Hands clasped neatly on the desk, I concentrate on Mr Beezley, who's bent so low over his desk that the class is presented with a balding globe. He is flicking the pencil between his thumb and forefinger as if it has a cigarette-ash end to get rid of. His fingers are nicotine stained. They rise, gripping the flat pencil-end, dragging it across his oranged pate.

'His nickname's Beacon Bonce,' she informs me. Amusement tickles my throat. But I will not be drawn in. I fill my head with the teacher's real name and rank: *Mr Beezley, Geography*.

Insinuating its way into my line of vision is a head of mad wire hair, that makes her look like she's been electrocuted at the temples.

'Gi' it a couple o' weeks,' rasps my skinny weed neighbour, 'an' it'll be more a scive than a lesson.'

It strikes me, how could she possibly have any idea? She must be new like me, and therefore equally ignorant.

85

'How could *you* know?' I whisper-challenge.

'Yer gets around; yer ask, yer listen,' she replies. Her eyes get an impish glint about them. She indicates to look down to where the table is shielded from the teacher. She's got a pack of cigarettes – Embassy Regal – which she's lightly shaking as if not sure if they're shock-material or delights to tempt.

'Yers smoke?'

I glance at the cigarettes with disdain. Seen *plenty* of those.

She shrugs her shoulders and grins.

Out of nowhere is a suppressed explosion of what threatens to be only the start of some kind of wheezing fit. Blood shoots into the whites of her popping-out eyes. Her mouth can't open wide enough.

I look to the teacher. His head's lowered further; his pencil rattling on the desk is loud enough to eliminate all other sounds around him.

My neighbour seems to be grappling for something in her skirt pocket. Her hand's shaking too much. I grapple for her. I extract a short metal tube, which her bird-claw hand grabs and yanks to her mouth. Even after her rattling skeleton collapse, the rapid-fire hissing sound of this tube squirting something into her mouth makes me jump.

She seems somewhat recovered.

'Ta,' she tries to quip jocularly. The thank you abbreviation is hardly as loud as the rustle of the one tree outside.

'Asthma,' she explains. I intend to tell her she's too worn out to be chatting. But she's jollying herself back into her stride, just slightly rasping now.

'My name's Heather, Heather Robinson. I'll be yer friend, if you want,' she offers simply.

I wriggle in my chair, uncomfortable.

The bell announcing the start of break is still screaming like an electric current round the school. I ought to wait for Karen where we said, at the corridor of lockers. Heather Robinson is running off, at a wheezing scuttle, to where the tarmac changes to cracked dirt that was once lawn. Now she's at the scraggy beech-bush fence that's been reinforced with super-strength crossed wire. She's bending down to where a triangle of wire has been worked away from the concrete post. Her popping eyes glance back to say I am invited. It's up to me.

I shouldn't follow.

I shove my plastic pencil-case tight inside my uniform skirt waistband, and I make a dash for it. My breathing speeds excitedly. As long as I'm quick enough so Karen doesn't see, I can lie that I was held back by the teacher.

Wriggle after Heather's bony ankle, and we're through.

We must cross a road. This is too like *really* sciving. I will be found out. Time for me to turn back. But Heather's grabbed my wrist and she is running.

What about the Green Cross Code? We must look right and left and right again, not presume the traffic will screech-stop.

My sensibleness is somewhere on the pavement far behind me. I *glare* at the driver who's doing the irate beeping. I didn't mean to!

My heart is in my mouth and ready to fall out. Still being dragged. I shut my eyes.

We've stopped. The traffic has receded, drowned out by sounds of water. I keep my eyes closed tight. I smell some kind of bitter vegetation. I hear Heather's inhaler hiss-pumping medication down her throat.

I swing my head round and look at her hard. I suppose even with my glasses and put-on scolding expression, I can't hide that I'm close to grinning.

'Yer like it, then?' she asks, almost apprehensive. 'It's t'weir.'

Normally I'd feel obliged to indicate with a 'tt' or a superior wavering of the eyebrow that any fool can see it's a weir. Not today.

We sit close together on the edge of the brick wall that drops down vertically to where the river changes – from a serene plateau to raging white froth and surging black caverns. It plummets far below to a gurgling, meandering level. We are surrounded by tall weeds which have beautiful pink flowers. I look back to where we stood. Crushed stalks ooze sticky white sap.

Heather takes out a cigarette and a box of matches. I don't even mind that she's going to smoke, because she brought me here. I do wonder if it's wise, though, seeing as she's got asthma. I pull myself up short. Her decision; nothing to do with me.

I go back to staring past my gently swinging rumply white-socked and Clarke-shoed feet, into the swirling dancing water. Cigarette smoke drifts past. I make sure to not breathe it in.

Heather is suddenly intently staring at me.

'Shall I show yer somethink?'

I only vaguely wonder what this something might be. It's like I am in the countryside where I can feel blank, nearly. Or, at least, not like any minute I could put my foot wrong and cause earth-shattering disasters. It's nice to realise I could hardly care less what Heather wants to show me. But then it's only polite to pretend.

'OK,' I chirp.

She clamps the cigarette between her teeth. The curling blue smoke makes her squinch up her eyes and wrinkle her pale forehead. I hear that she's grappling past the inhaler in her skirt pocket. She brings out a small rectangular paper packet. It's a bit like the miniature salt packets at the take-away bit of Harry Ramsden's, only it has gold writing on.

I shrug my shoulders obligingly.

''S a condom,' she says, the words clumsy round her teeth-clamped cigarette.

Con-dom.

I wait for her to carry on.

She rips the package open. She unfurls something pink and floppy with globby bits of slime on. She removes the cigarette with a triumphant flourish, breathes out smoke – with a bit of a raspy cough – and dangles this latex object in front of us.

'It's fer sex,' she says.

Now sex I know about: a man and a woman marry and have babies. She doesn't have to waste her time explaining.

I say this. Her reaction is, to say the least, offensive. She laughs so hard she has to scrabble for her inhaler. I won't help her find it.

After a couple of medication inhalations, she looks apologetic for her mirth – quite right too! – and says with a straight face how the man's penis, only she incorrectly calls it willy, goes hard like rock.

I consider becoming prissily aloof again. It seems ungrateful. I try to get involved with her description.

Does she mean the penis is like a stick of rock, I wonder, or stone rock? She supposes it's like stick rock, only thicker. And then it gets inserted in this plastic, here.

My patience suddenly is gone.

For a start that condom is only a flimsy thing. And as for some penis bigger than stick rock going up inside a woman . . .

It's just plain silly. Heather's joking me.

I smile, testingly. She shrugs her shoulders.

'I cud help yers, y'know. Learn yer things,' she says.

■

I leave the main bedroom light off and direct the pool of anglepoise light on to today's diary page.

Tuesday 9 p.m.

Issue: the importance of solitude

It involved a lot of attention-seeking – all those nit-bitty quarrels with Phyll. It was well worth it.

Now I have MY OWN ROOM. It's not the nicest in the world, but it's MINE.

'Dad. I need my own room.'

I decided the best way was to announce it as a *fait accompli*, stood behind him while he was working, so it would be more effort to interrogate me than just say yes. His hand gripping the pen was fidgeting off and on to the page. His shoulders were hunching further over his desk, because, I know, he didn't want to argue about why I suddenly felt I needed my own room, or where I bloody well thought I might have it.

I declared into the air above the back of his head as matter of factly as was possible, 'I'll move into the room off the kitchen.'

His pen stopped. His back went like an electric fence.

And just then, as if she knew what I was doing, upstairs on the landing Phyll must have pushed Max – the usual effortless hand into the face that sends Max flying – because there was a crash against the wall followed by enraged scufflings: Phyll holding Max at arm's length by the head; him flailing wildly with his arms and legs and not getting anywhere near her.

I could sympathise with Dad's position. It's infuriating being in a fight, but it's worse to listen to.

The fight-scuffling got louder, sounding to Dad like me and Phyll must do when he's trying to watch telly.

'Fine. Move rooms,' he snapped. Then, his eyebrows knotted so much they pushed his glasses skew-whiff. His head tilted back. He bellowed full volume up at the ceiling, 'Shut the fuck up!'

Sulky silence from Phyll and Max. Dad dug his pen back into the paper.

'Tell me when you've cleaned it out,' he muttered angrily.

It didn't hit me immediately, the reality of moving into the room off the kitchen which we didn't go into because of it being mum's. I felt my chin hit my chest. My hands flapped loose at my sides. I folded them into purposeful fists. I snapped my head back up, because I had a busy schedule ahead: cleaning, painting, furniture-moving. All the same, when it came to it, on the stone step at the back of the kitchen, I stood with the scrubbing-brush in my hand for a long time before I could make myself lift the latch.

After she'd left, before the men came with the removals van to take her things away, me and Phyll and Max had gone in once. We'd climbed over the damp-warped cardboard boxes and tea-chests, stamping, aiming for breakages. We'd stood at the far end in front of her piano, and we wrote Dad's name on the keys. We'd taken it in turns to each do a letter in indelible, black, marker pen: M-A-R-T-I-N B-E-N-N-E-T-T.

Max hadn't ever meant to do anything wrong when he started keeping his action man under the lid of mum's piano. He'd only laid it out for safe-keeping from me and Phyll. He didn't know it could do damage to the strings and felt-covered hammers. But she'd raged at Max – about not wanting to have to buy crap all her life just to allow for us ruining her things.

We let Max do the last defacing 'T' on the keys of her piano.

We never looked in the room after.

I decided that plenty of time had passed. There would be lots of dust and cobwebs and no evidence **91** of her things. I was wrong. There was a two tier dust system: thinner, in ghost square markings where boxes and tea chests had been. The floorboards still sagging at the end where her piano was.

But it's *my* room now.

I stuck my heels together, splayed my feet and swished them furiously from one end to the other so *my mark* zigzagged through the dust all the way across. I opened the window. Dust blew into my hair, eyes, nose, mouth. My eyes streamed. I retched and coughed and spat the taste out. I hurled the bucket of water over the floor. The black wetness cut the dust off at source. Gusts of wind sucked out the dirt particles that swirled under the ceiling. I dropped on my knees too fast, bruising, and I scrubbed, harder, harder every inch of every floorboard.

I don't suppose that's how it's meant to be done, without soap. I only moved the dirt into an even coating. I didn't actually clean. But I did remove the marks.

The paint was stuff left over in the barn. Weather protection. Metallic red. It makes the room small. The walls seem to close in on me. It feels when I'm lying down as if the ceiling will come lower and lower and squash me flat.

But there's no evidence of where family photographs were hung up.

'Dad. I'm done.'

I'd started when it was light. I caught my reflection in the back door window when I'd finished: dust-coloured all over; mad red eyes; hair sticking out all over the place like I'd seen a ghost.

Dad didn't notice. He practically threw the spare bunk bed from Max's room in. His head was turned looking the other way when he did it.

No-one but me comes in my room. I like it that way. After they've all gone to bed, I'm on my own at the back of the house. I don't get involved with anyone else's problems. And, that way, soon I won't have to have any of my own.

Conclusion: solitude is a nearly achieved and desirable state.

I don't care if night-time frost is setting in. It is bracing with the window open.

My fingers on the desk are numb. Self-hate is slicing into my head.

Ah! That's bare feet I hear on the stone tiles in the kitchen. I'll bet it's Max, coming to *whine* about the way I got his bunk. I'm glad I left the door ajar. I can taunt by letting him see into my room, then from my haughty distance in this bentwood chair I will refuse him entry. I might make him whine so loud he'll get told off.

The door is being crashed open. It's Phyll filling up the doorframe. My heart is palpitating like it has no casing. I hurl myself against my wooden plank barrier; my fingers fight to get the latch locked into place.

I know I was wrong to make the quarrels with her just to get my own room. I didn't realise she'd care so much. My intestines twist from yearning. But I *cannot* let her in – there is my *private* diary still left out on the desk.

'Get out!' I clench the words to stop myself from screaming out in panic.

She has no *right*! How *dare* she be ungrateful. I conceded her the best room, without even being petty by telling her I was doing her a favour. She has the room with the view over fields that cascade into the valley. I took the cell.

Her shoulder barging is too strong. She grabs my arm – my school-uniformed arm. Her fingers dig until she is at my bone. In this shirt I am supposed to be invincible!

'Let me in,' she demands.

I can't accept it's fear I have at the way her eyes volcano fury from behind her screen of hair. She *shan't* bully me with her strength. She can't make me need her.

'At Big School they will get out knives and hack that stupid fringe off,' I hiss. She's unnerved just long enough for me to twist my arm out of her grip.

The wood planks smash into the frame. I've shut her out.

Flat against the door, with all my weight pulled down on the latch, I feel spiteful.

I am suddenly, desperately, shivery.

■

I can't accept Heather Robinson liking me, not even in the relative secrecy of class. How would it be productive? In no way. That's come extra clear to me now, standing here in the school-dinner queue, directly behind Karen Crawley.

How could I fade into the background with Heather needing me to scrabble to get her inhaler all the time? My point was proved exactly. 'You'd only show me up,' I declared coldly. She went and had a wheezing fit from hurt.

It makes me cringe that I felt swelled by self-satisfied malice. She really did want me as her friend. And now I've shut myself off from the peace of the weir. But it *was* necessary to scorn her.

With Karen, there is no room for misunderstanding. I will be her side-kick; she will be my barrier.

Banana enamel hair grips and frilly shirts . . . those are distant memories. Even her hair colour is going different. '*Sun-in,*' Karen says like she's an advertisement: '*Just spray and blow-dry and I'm blonder.*'

I stand quietly behind Karen Crawley and no one takes any notice whatsoever. My tie-knot stays pea-sized and I watch Karen show off a new development each day: two inch platforms; then rust blusher; then lip gloss . . .

Today in the dinner queue, Karen Crawley keeps tossing her head back, which is a bit annoying, seeing as I'm so close. I am getting the full impact of what she's trying to show off. It's spiking me: her laquered hair. She's mainly concentrated on getting lots on. Her hair's solid. It does look daft. But it wins her status, and the more status Karen has, the more I'm left unbothered. Which is perfect.

The dinner queue inches forwards. The smells are seeming to separate. I am engulfed in the compost odour of overcooked broccoli. I am buffeted by Smash chemical fluffiness.

Creeping in further behind Karen Crawley has a triple benefit. She takes the full brunt of the wafting dinner; I get several safe inches back from the laquered hair she's still tossing pointedly; and – veiled by the queue of pupils – I am freed to look around. For a start, I'm quite curious about the way Karen has folded the sides of her hairstyle back into infant sculpted flicks. I wonder how long it will take before they've grown to be the regulation stiff ear flaps. And what is the dividing line between the ear flaps and the *really* massive flicks that swing independently, like on that new girl, who's standing in the centre of the stretched horizontal dinner hall steps like she's about to make an announcement.

Her hair flicks are bigger than humanly looks possible, and they are not just blonde: they are white peroxide. They are so thickly laquered that the chemicals have crystallised. They glitter, almost like she's wearing a crown.

I suppose Karen senses my attention's on something other than her. The two patches of rust blusher are turned hard towards me then towards the object of my gaze. Annoyance is replaced by contempt.

'Tha's Bev Grant,' she says, her peach-glossed **95**

top lip curling. 'Didn't yer know? 'Er Dad's an alcoholic. She 'as to 'ave *deprived children's* dinner tickets.'

Karen's queue neighbours one by one stop betting what today's spam variation will be. Karen says, rather louder than is necessary for just me to hear, 'Yer don't wanna get too close ter someone like Bev Grant. Yer don't know what yer might catch.'

Now most of the dinner queue is staring at Bev Grant.

Bev lifts one six-inch platformed shoe up a step, menacingly. Karen says, 'She's 'ad to change schools five times because of 'er Dad's drinkin'.'

Bev Grant thrusts her chest out. The tight T-shirt material is stretched to snapping point. I think even Karen is impressed by the sheer hugeness of this bust. But the queue conspires to send a Chinese whisper up and down the queue, '*She's* t' one wi' *nits*'. Then, the worst snub, everyone ignores her. The general subject for discussion returns to what the dinner-ladies have in store for us.

Bev Grant's eyes are extremely clogged with mascara, so it's hard to tell, but I suspect the flashing indicates she will not accept this treatment. If she's changed schools five times, she must have been through this a lot, this working out what she needs to do in order to establish herself in the pupil hierarchy. She must be sick of messing about.

Pupils Chinese whisper up the queue that the spam's not frittered today. It's spam curry. The whole queue wishes it wasn't. Everyone's busy condemning the kitchen staff for lack of imagination when Bev Grant announces coolly, 'I'm goin' ter . . . '

Her knuckle-dusting ringed fingers position themselves in attack-mode fists on her hips. She surveys the queue with an expression as if she has taken everyone's contempt and is sending it back at them in multiplied

intensity.

'I', she says again, not even needing to raise her voice, 'am goin' ter get pregnant . . . '

Children nudge their mates and whisper, conspiratorial and giggly, in each other's ears. After all, teenage pregnancy's not a big deal at this school.

'I'll get pregnant by a married man.' *Married* man? They're usually teenage boys, who stand by them. 'I'll go through wi' it alone, an' I'll 'ave t' baby adopted.'

Adopted! The whole dinner-queue is staring at Bev Grant, agog. Spam curry suddenly seems unimportant. We don't quite know how to receive Bev's news. It's an interesting tactic that she's decided to announce the shock beforehand.

But Karen Crawley is no fool. She spots the catch: 'When?' she demands to know. 'When are yer goin' ter do this then? Go on, tell us!' Others join in: 'Yeah, when? When, then?'

She can't get pupil hierarchy respect *that* easily. Unless Bev Grant is prepared to give a precise time-table of events, they say she is not to be trusted. 'We don't believe yer!' they taunt.

'I'll do it all within t' year.'

Jaws drop further. Eyebrows rise higher. She really means it. Bev's thin smile suggests that she is satisfied. We are in awe.

More than that, I am somewhat horrified. Surely this is rather drastic action just to get attention.

Like an automaton, I follow Karen Crawley along the stainless steel food-runway with my tray and plate, having items splatted on. I feel someone should tell Bev Grant she doesn't really have to do it. I look to Paul Cragg at the back. I don't think he knows how to respond. He does make sure to smile reassurance at Bev Grant, but it's a shaky smile, and anyway she's not looking.

Her flicks, fallen forwards, have turned into bleached blinkers. She's on her way outside to the quad. She sits on a weather-beaten box-bench by a bin.

In the stifling dinner-hall, I sit at a hexagonal formica table. My prissily tight-knotted sky-blue-and-navy tie clashes violently with the cubed spam curry.

In full view of the dinner hall's long, flat windows, Bev Grant slides a cigarette between the middle- and index-fingers of her right hand. The chipped pink varnish on her bitten nails reflect the sun. When she lights the cigarette, she sucks in hard and her brown-blushered cheeks collapse. Then she exhales and squeezes the packet back into her left breast pocket.

Suddenly I can't bear to be sitting next to Karen Crawley. She holds her knife and fork as if they are diamond-headed knitting needles. Just shove them in the food and eat! That's all they're for. But Karen Crawley always knows what's *proper*.

She has flicks and platforms just the same as Bev Grant. What makes Karen's not *common*?

Over there – he's so infuriating – Paul Cragg. I suppose he thinks he's clever, standing alone all the time, not bothering that he's right at the back of the dinner queue.

Every so often he gives me one of his looks, with eyes that are unnervingly clear. It's like he knows how I can't stand Karen Crawley, and how I treated Heather Robinson.

I *haven't* compromised. I've merely come to a convenient arrangement.

Anyway, I have other things to think about than him or Karen or Bev Grant. For example, not letting my mind wander while I'm supposed to be concentrating on immediates, like food. As pleased as I am with my brazenly obedient tight tie-knot, it strikes me, as I glance down, that there may, after all, be something to be said for following trends. If my tie were loose and wide, the tongue would not have just trailed in my dinner. The brown sauce looks particularly revolting against the pale blue stripes.

It's Maths straight after lunch. Wigley will have a field-day. He'll probably say something sarcastic like: 'If we'd known we had pigs for pupils we'd have supplied troughs instead of tables.'

Even *I* don't sit at the front for Wigley's class if I can help it. I'd almost like to retract my nastiness to Heather so we could be allies.

The first lesson with Wigley, I thought it was just a one-off scare tactic; now I know it's just the way he is. We all file in. Some teachers stand, others sit in a chair, but he's always sitting on the top of the front desk in his baggy green-checked suit, his legs wrapped round behind his head.

He rocks a little on his haunches and frowns while he waits for us to settle. Then he unwinds his legs, springs off the table and grabs Andrew Pennington by the scruff of the neck, all in one movement. He drags a pupil to the front. He asks a question from the homework. The panic on its own is enough to send the answer scooting from the pupil's head. They say, 'Don't know, sir.' Mr Wigley bellows, 'You don't know? You *don't know*! Face the blackboard.' Then he says, 'No. I want you closer to the wall. Closer. *Closer.*' He takes hold of their hair – to get a good swing – and bangs his head against the wall.

Once Mr Wigley has established that violence is mightier than reason, he sends the pupil back to their seat, red-faced and shaking. Mr Wigley is entirely calm and composed.

They're certainly not pleasant, Mr Wigley's lessons. But I know I won't be victimised. I'm the only studious-acting one in the class. At Utley comprehensive, I have control.

1976

We have been summoned to the kitchen, as if because we're brother and sisters we're automatically linked. On this freezing winter evening, we are an unwilling trio, Max, Phyll and I.

Reluctantly, though, a bit of me is quite touched by Dad's behaviour. He's nervous. For once in a blue moon he takes notice of what I look like.

'Allie, hmm.' He knots his brows. 'Those clothes appear to be getting rather small for you.'

Certainly, this bee-stripe jumper is slicing my armpits, and the hems of my turquoise corduroys are flaring at the calves instead of the ankles. But I'm only saving *his* money, by making sure I keep my school uniform pristine and not asking for new weekend clothes.

Anyway, I don't know why what *I'm* wearing is such a big deal to Dad in the first place. He's got on his million-years-old tatty black polo-neck. Just because it has a dark-coloured T-shirt underneath so the jumper's holes don't show, and just because he's damped his hair down doesn't mean he looks smart. I suppose this strikes him too as we hear a car spray gravel at a speed that indicates it's careering unwisely fast into the yard. It looks like he can't decide whether to smile or panic.

Neither of these expressions sit easily with the frown lines that are etched into his face. He stands directly in front of us. He stretches down his arms to clasp me by my right shoulder and Max by his left so he can encourage us nearer to each other, each closer to Phyll in the middle. We resist, stubbornly gripping our bare feet to the cold stone floor. He can make us be in a line in the kitchen, but he can't dictate the distance between us. Even if he manages, by physical force, we'll just spring apart later. But he suddenly stops bothering to try.

He has focused on us I see, to give himself time to get collected. He's securing his non-committal grave expression. I almost want his attention back. I mind that he eases open the back door with unprecedented quiet and precision. This new carefulness is not for us. Ice wind lashes into the kitchen, making us hop our bare feet. 'I will,' he announces, 'be back shortly.'

He's only going as far as the yard, for God's sake.

He pulls the door to behind him and the outside light glares his eyes. His brows close in over his spectacles as he marches, apparently purposefully but in fact unbelievably slow-motion, towards the flagged path between the two raised flower-beds.

The second he's gone, I make sure to be the first to get a snidey dig in. I am separate from them. At twelve, I am getting close to adult.

Phyll is just about to slip her two fingers and thumb into her mouth. I tilt my head right back so I can look down my nose at her superiorly.

'They kick children's heads in for sucking their thumb at Big School,' I call up at her primly. She snaps her hand back down to her side and shapes it ominously **101** into a fist. She tells me she doesn't care *what* they think of her at Big School, but I know she's becoming scared.

'You'll have to get a *lot* more *mature* if you're going to last two minutes,' I say obnoxiously.

The trick with Phyll is knowing when to stop. As glowering turns the pupils lurking in her hooded eyes to black poisoned darts, as her huge and getting bigger shoulders begin to swivel in my direction, I start in on Max.

'Of course, at Big School, they'll think your freckles are *pimples*,' I tell him. 'They'll pour bleach in the toilet then flush your head down.'

I gauge my power by if I can get his squint going even now they've done the hospital operation that cured it. Yes. Max's eyeball muscles resist the stitches that pulled them back into place. His blue irises cloud over and move, only slightly but very definitely closer to the bridge of his nose.

'Of course,' I sneer, secure in my position as bossy older sister, 'now you're squinting Dad'll *know* you're tired and you'll have to go to bed early, *again*.'

'*Not* tired,' asserts Max.

'Are.'

'*Aren't*.'

I have got them going like they are warring minions at my command. Phyll is still glowering between us. Max sticks his skinny goose-bumped arm out from its T-shirted sleeve to poke his aggravation into my ribs. Over-her-head volleys are fine, but Phyll will not tolerate Max's petulant across-her-midriff fisticuffs. She bats him off her as easily as if he's a fly. She swings her arm to bash me too for good measure, but I've already leapt away.

'Missed!' I hiss.

She'd take one giant stride over and bash me proper, only – my timing was perfect – we hear whispers outside, somewhere around the bottom of the flagstone path that leads between the raised up flower-beds to the house.

Instantly, we are united. So what if it's to do with loneliness and fear? Phyll and Max and I have a family hierarchy to protect.

There've been *other* female colleagues. This one's not the first, and if she thinks we'll treat her specially, she's got another thing coming.

It's of no consequence if they spend the night in Dad's bed. Especially when they're stupid enough to think we don't know. We couldn't not, since we get *woken up* by the colleagues stumbling at some God-awful hour from his room to the guest-room next door, all for the sake of pretending the next morning they were there all along. The guest bed's never *nearly* crumpled enough to be convincing. And anyway, it's far too cold. I took all but one of the covers for my own bed. They'd freeze if they really slept there. They must think we're idiots.

I can see Phyll and Max have been thinking the same thing, because we all straighten our backs defiantly and stretch our necks as high as possible, in unison. We place our arms militaristically at our sides – to make it clear we're *under* orders to be here – and we fix our expressions at vaguely quizzical, with a twist to the eyebrow that indicates we know she won't last long. *All* our eyes have poisoned darts in.

We watch intently Dad's black jumper curtaining over the outside of the back door window as he leans across to grasp the handle. The metal curve creaks down; his arm flings the door open. He stands back, and we are facing a figure who's tall and – annoyingly – imposing, largely because we can't make out any features. Whoever it is, they are silhouetted in the doorway by the outdoor light, sleet glancing lightly off them then slicing cold into the kitchen. We cannot stop our shivering now. We hunch up together and deep **103** breathe fast for warmth, which entirely destroys our nightmare-children-from-hell look, while this stranger has a damned good chance to inspect us long and hard.

Why doesn't Dad make this colleague come in now? Him standing out there in the background, meekly holding her suitcase, while we're being blasted by cold weather straight off the moor.

It's not until we are feeling really *extremely* silly that the colleague finally decides to step into the kitchen. Me, Max and Phyll, one frozen unit, are still trying to keep our faces in of-course-you-won't-last-long sort of expressions. Mainly, though, while Dad closes the door and we wait to thaw, we're curious. I am pretty angry that she already won a battle of wills, before I'd even seen her face, but I'm also in a way impressed.

The other colleagues rushed in, all effusiveness and lying, armed with compliments and gifts to win us over. This one appears to have no presents. She's not attempting to introduce herself. She is shamelessly still surveying us, eyebrows raised imperiously, over the top of a pair of half glasses that have steamed up in the relative heat of the kitchen. Her eyes are small and neat, dark chocolate coloured irises surrounded by thick lashes that sparkle with melted sleet.

I recall my mood: I shove my forefinger up the bridge of my nose to secure *my* glasses, which are bigger and better than hers, and not stupid half-glasses that are all for show.

Her lips are sticky out sullen, although it seems from Dad's expression that this is by no means un-appealing. He tries to pretend everything's like normal, but he can't look anywhere but at this colleague. Neither can we, because we can't believe she hasn't weakened yet and tried to ingratiate herself.

Quite the contrary. It's with an objectionably relaxed flourish that she takes off her charcoal beret and shakes out a mane of glossy jet-black hair. With wool, multi-coloured striped gloved fingers, she swiftly unbuttons her huge man's overcoat, and tosses it lightly into the wicker chair beneath the telephone – where Dad usually chucks his coat – and then she tosses her gloves on top, which is really pushing it. But Dad's only showing awed fascination.

She's wearing a polo-neck under another jumper, *and* a cardigan over the top. This is excellent ammunition. She's soft. I regret not having only a T-shirt on like Max, to show how *hard* we are up here, but still – bare feet's a good touch.

I suppose that she's from a cosmopolitan southern town, or maybe even a *city*. She won't last seconds. I bet she's never seen *real* snow, been weather-bound by seven-foot drifts and had to put plastic bags inside her walking boots for waterproofing. Those shoes don't look sturdy enough to pass as slippers, and in this house we think slippers are for *weak* people.

She surprises us all by speaking suddenly. We expect something sugary in our direction.

'Martin,' she calls back at Dad in a voice that hums and rolls melodically on just a single word. 'You *could* turn up the central heating.'

How dare she? This is one of Dad's ways of economising. But he mumbles, 'Christ – is it freezing? Terribly sorry,' and he's scrabbling about in the coat cupboard for the central-heating knob. I can't believe he's bowing to her.

The boiler roars ominously and pipes rattle as Dad re-emerges, his hair all in disarray and his body skewed with having the colleague's suitcase in one hand and the other still holding on to the central-heating control panel in the coat cupboard for balance.

The colleague's eyes are directed impatiently towards a remote corner of the kitchen ceiling in a way that indicates she's waiting for Dad to take the initiative.

'Ah, of course.' His words stumble out clumsily. 'Let me – ah – introduce you to, urrmm, my children.' Using the suitcase as a pointer, he names us each by turn – 'Allie, Phyll, Max' – again with something that touchingly resembles pride. I don't know why. We're still goose-bumped and blue-lipped, and we may not look like we're from hell anymore, but we do look like children from a place that most people would go to some lengths to avoid.

Undeterred, the colleague does a cursory glance at each of us in turn. Her hands are on her hips in a self-containing sort of a way. She's not having any attempt to shake our hands or kiss our cheeks or anything like that. Her eyes are scouring us, yet she manages to hum her name to us almost absent-mindedly: 'Scarlet Barr.'

It is clear to me suddenly that she has put little or possibly no thought beforehand into what she'd do when she met us. I find that this is extremely irritating, and to even find it irritating is irritating in itself. Why should she matter to me one way or the other? I feel myself bristling and thrusting my angry head forwards.

Scarlet Barr considers, apparently for a mere split second, how to get through this dreadful evening of introductions.

We are prepared to be insolent.

Her voice rolls alluringly. 'Shall we . . . '

Our sneers say that nothing *she* has to suggest will be of interest to us.

She says, 'Shall we play poker.'

Dad drops her suitcase. Poker? Colleagues aren't supposed to ask children – not *Dad's* children – if they want to play poker. Dad is horrified. We practically choke. That's *gambling.*

But then Phyll and Max and I realise what's going on. She's playing a very cheap trick. She's being unconventional on *purpose*. I fold my arms and stare annoyedly at the ceiling. Max and Phyll do their bored can't-we-go-now look in Dad's direction.

Colleague Scarlet Barr's busy acting looking around her in surprise. 'You do,' she asks the room, '*have* a pack of cards, I suppose.'

Phyll, Max and I swivel our heads to investigate the honesty of the expression on her face. Her eyebrows are up so high they're practically beyond her hair line. She really does want to play poker.

Out of stubborn pride, I'm reluctant to respond. Max, though, is as near as I've ever seen him get to bubbling over with excitement. Has he forgotten about loyalty towards us? He steps forwards and tugs at her jumper's sleeve.

'I'll get the cards,' he whispers up her arm.

He is only young. It might confuse her having one person act a little bit nicely towards her. But no.

'Good,' Scarlet Barr says simply, apparently not at all understanding what this fuss is about. I guess she thinks if she has to spend an evening with three children, she may as well get a game of poker out of it. Perhaps that is a way I should look at it too. It might be fun doing something Dad doesn't want us to.

He grumphs awkwardly that he won't be playing. He has some work he really ought to be getting on with. Scarlet Barr is not at all put out. She shrugs her shoulders exaggeratedly as if to say he can suit himself. Then her eyes begin to show the hint of a smile, and she winks her eye at him – I'm not sure that I approve of this. I'm not sure he approves either. He looks gobsmacked then embarrassed as he goes so fast he's almost running to get ensconced in his desk.

The kitchen's a hopeless plan – too near Dad. We must play in the sitting-room.

I say to the colleague Scarlet Barr, as imperiously as possible, 'Follow me, please.' I make 'please' into a command instead of politeness and I won't deign to **107** look at her so it is abundantly clear that I am not defeated. I am just going along with things for a while to see how they develop.

Phyll lopes along behind. Nothing is going to stop her slipping her two fingers and thumb into her mouth now. This is too strange, a colleague who doesn't realise that using the sitting-room for anything other than Dad's late-night television is a major breakthrough.

I creak open the plank door and, with as much coldness as I can muster, I usher Scarlet Barr in, and then I think *damn*, because there's only the one decent armchair, and she'll sit in it and feel superior. But I can't be seen to run to it in defensive panic.

Max ducks under my arm and dashes in with the pack. He crashes down, knees and elbows first on to the middle of the floor and starts sorting out the cards to be all face down. We hear Dad's swivel-chair creak as he sits down and scrapes it across the tiles to be nearer his desk.

To buy myself time, I concentrate on how Scarlet Barr is surveying the room from under her lashes. She suddenly removes her half glasses and puts them in her trouser pocket. 'Atmosphere,' she murmurs and strides elegantly yet with purpose over to the anglepoise Dad has by the armchair in case he wants to work while he's watching telly. Scarlet Barr unceremoniously moves it and sticks its head in the stone fireplace. 'Lights!' she declares to Phyll. *Nobody* orders Phyll around like that – but she's entranced like Max. It is an unspoken agreement between us three that she is antagonistic to every stranger. With not so much as a mini-glower, she switches off the main light. It is up to me I suppose now. But I'm losing the sharpness of the urge to subvert.

The chipped orange anglepoise reflects off the stone a dusky glow that goes nowhere near the cob-webs or the cigarette burns in the armchair or the uncomfortableness of the spiky bits on the wire-hessian carpet. The sitting-room looks almost romantic.

I close the door, delaying, my eyes focused on my shuffling feet while I work fuzzily on the question of how to not let Scarlet Barr be higher than me on the chair. Perhaps I can introduce an extra one from the kitchen.

I look up, and am nonplussed.

She is sinking gracefully into a casual cross-legged position, next to Max, *on the floor*. Furthermore, she is not even bothering to wait for me before she starts. I rush over and plonk myself down, fast as lightning, between Phyll and Scarlet Barr.

I am in danger of becoming entranced too.

Scarlet Barr's silver-ringed fingers are flashing in and out, shuffling faster than ought to be humanly possible. It's amazing the cards don't just spray out round the room.

She's muttering about them being damaged. Too many violent games of snap, when we *bash* each other's hands for victory by submission. But I won't tell her that; childish. Instead, I rouse myself and determine to get a snidey gibe in – have another go at getting her off her stride.

'What are *they*?' I ask, pointing at the pair of feetless rainbow-coloured socks she has pulled up over her fawn slacks. I try to make my voice intimate how much she would be ridiculed at Big School for this item of dress. If I succeed, she doesn't mind one bit. She looks up at me, silver rings still flashing, and says coolly, 'They're leg-warmers. Any more questions or can we get on with the game?'

I feel the size of an ant that's just been stood on. That's supposed to be *my* job, doing it to Phyll and Max! And at least I do it in private.

'Go ahead,' I mumble and do a buttock-shuffle back away from the spotlighting anglepoise.

'Now. The significance of damaged cards,' she declares.

Her voice has a sing-song to it. Despite my under-mined position, it soothes me in the soft-lighted room as she talks about how professional gamblers would memorise what damage each card had and so win by cheating.

I find it is getting hard to keep in mind about winding her up while she explains how to play – murmuring about flushes and runs and full houses, and, most important of all, she says, poker-faces.

That is no problem. Since starting at big school, I have a permanent poker-face. It is essential.

Tonight, I suppose I will lose, because I am finding it is not possible to stop my expression from relaxing. I am so used to my jaw being rigid like it is stuck with dynamite, it feels uncomfortably loose the way my face skin is not taut and my lips are parting. I should shut them. I fear I am, against my better judgement, beginning to perhaps even enjoy myself.

Don't undress properly – stumble into bed – too tired to do the diary, or even close the wood-bits blind.

Don't mind the cold tonight. Kick the covers; blow hot on to my ice fingers. Watch outside the window where sleet has turned to soft floating particles of snow.

Scarlet Barr with flashing rings and stripey leg-warmers and lots of shaggy black hair that helps her poker-face because it screens her when she's looking at her hand. Swishing and swooshing the cards in dizzying whirls and not being able to hide her pleasure when she wins even though we're only children.

She was the most fun of the fleeting colleagues. She taught us poker. Scarlet Barr will be a fond memory. I might almost miss her.

Scarlet Barr.

She is an actress. She has insinuated her way into our lives and I hate her.

She thinks she has control. She doesn't know that where I am, standing outside here in the dark in the mud and gorse of the back field, I can see everything she's doing.

Rehearsing for a thee-*etter* production.

Lit up glowing in the upstairs window, she is flouncing to and fro with bits of paper held high. Her eyebrows arch regally.

That used to be the guest-room. Cold. Cobwebbed. All of a sudden it's her *workroom*. And everyone else has to act like they're non-existent so as to not disturb her.

Coned in his desk anglepoise, Dad downstairs doesn't move his swivel chair. Phyll and Max sitting at the kitchen table doing homework aren't allowed to ask to pass a pencil. They don't even try to rebel.

Out here I *kick* at a marshy clump of reeds.

She talks to Dad about 'symbolism' in Shakespeare. She comes and goes when it suits *her* timetable, sometimes mid-week. It was one of Dad's rules. Work and school are paramount. Now that's except when Scarlet Barr's concerned. I wish she'd bugger off and leave us alone, like we were before.

Even Mrs Taylor is a traitor. When I asked her, she was standing at the sink. The way she put down her cloth and crossed her soapy arms, I was sure she'd be on my side. She didn't like the other 'colleagues'. She pursed her lips and mulled her eyebrows up and down to keep me guessing before finally she pronounced, 'I like her.' The Scottish 'r' of 'her' rolled on and on insulting.

I dig my Clarke-shoed, unsocked feet into freezing

cold marsh ground. I hunch down and thrust my hands in too. The intensity of the minus temperature makes my joints and head ache. It's all *her* fault.

I know it won't reach from so far back here in the field, but I grab up ice-mud and *hurl* it at this Scarlet Barr framed posing in the upstairs glass panes. Like a phutting firework only black and light inversed, the mud spray-dissipates before the brightness flooding from the guest-room window.

I shiver and feel pointless.

But here is tabby Benjamin, with his purring amber-glowing eyes all worried, trotting loyally towards me over reeds and clods of earth.

Stupid cat. I hate you too.

'*Bugger off!*'

I hurl mud and stones with one hand, both hands, more, faster, shell-blitzing all around him, and *laugh* as he streaks off out of sight towards the moor.

I can't sleep. I'm too angry. I turn over and fidget and twist on to my back.

Upstairs there is a thud: Max has fallen off his bunk. This is my chance.

Suddenly I am running, my body kept low and bent like a shadow through the house. I take three stairs at a time. It is tremulously like my lungs might burst, the way they're over-filling in my effort to not make noise by breathing.

Damn Max's screeching rusty hinges! Get it over; push the door fast open. My hand is stone on the latch. My heart hammers unbalancing from head to feet to guts till finally, it's back in place. No-one woke. Not even Max, judging by the silence.

My eyes strain, confused by being widely staring but seeing only blackness. Is that slightly blacker rectangle Max's bunk? The charcoal mound nearby, is that Max where he hurled himself to the bare boards in his sleep? I could feel nearly sorry for him.

Except I've watched him prancing out to the car, puppy-eagerly ahead of Dad, to meet *her*, Scarlet Barr. But he doesn't get what he wants. Sure, they can't do that sticky, sucky kissing because Max is gripping on her leg. But Dad's *affection* won't be shifted. They just wish Max'd bugger off. And that rumple Scarlet Barr's hand did once in Max's hair, it didn't *mean* anything. It was accident. Or maybe annoyance. Not friendliness.

I giant-step nearer, hoping a quaking plank will nightmare him into childish panic.

'Max!'

I intend to sound extremely bossy. My voice ricochets in the dark.

I crash the window open. Stinging wet hails on to my cheeks. I devil-laugh inside my head that this cold pain is what will make Max conscious. From the floor, I hear breathing noises that are satisfactorily disturbed.

'*Dad* should have come in here to see if you're OK,' I whisper to provoke him.

I want his whine. Dad can't just lock himself in bed with Scarlet Barr and think we'll go away.

But it must be Max's burdensome complaining. *He* will be responsible for bulldozing Scarlet Barr and Dad's intimacy, and that will be my revenge for Max's disloyalty.

Blurring black tells me his body's shuffling to escape the sleet.

'Max,' I persist, '*Dad* should be lifting you back on your bunk.'

But I've lost control. I am sounding desperate.

'Max!' My tone is coming out in the immature complaining I despise in him. I'm swirling to hysterical. I'm shaking him, wildly, viciously, to *force* him to comply.

'Stop it!' he says, suddenly cross.

113

It's like I have been slapped.

'Dad never comes,' he tells me as if I am a half-wit.

I feel like screaming that he should want her out as much as I do.

He mutters, 'Why did you have to go and wake me up?' as he climbs back into bed.

I am furious.

'You are *pathetic*,' I hiss, 'and *useless*.'

I turn my back on him. He probably can't even see my infantile gesture of rejection. I'm shaking. He whispers through the darkness, 'Allie?' His voice is adultly conciliating. I am shameful. 'Will you stay with me for a few minutes?'

How can he declare his need so simply?

Over by the doorway, I slide hopeless down the wall. I yank my knees up and collapse my head into their bone.

It's just because I happen to be here. Max doesn't want *me*. He wants Dad. He would maybe even rather be comforted by Scarlet Barr.

I am overwhelmed. Wetness floods my face.

■

Max and Phyll can do what they want. I will eject Scarlet Barr.

Considering my objective, this afternoon is underminingly sunny. But it is not hot. I yank off my mud-encrusted coat. The wind from the moor braces me. I will *not* degenerate to pleasant wooziness.

I keep it frozen solid in my mind that Dad devised this routine Sunday walk *for us Bennetts*, as an ideal method of combining exercise plus a quota of inter-family sociability. That's inter-*family*. Scarlet Barr is tagging on merely because I have been too tolerant. She and her two associates, Timothy and Roberto, should consider themselves bloody lucky to be here at all.

Not for long.

I won't slow my side-stitching pace. Even if it risks Dad lashing out for grinding my boots down on his heels, I'll force him to his usual grim determination speed in front of me.

I can feel from Phyll's breath on my neck that she is staying loyal to the old family unit, sticking excluding close behind me. And Max – I despise his fickleness – will keep with whoever gives him most attention. I turn, just for the brief time it takes to click my tongue to him, like he is some brainless animal. He trots firmer into line.

We are nearly at the second gate, a relentless unit filing fast upwards to the moor. I look back beyond Max's adrenalin-flushed face. My eyes detail every inch of wire-grassed field; my guts cheer the black-faced sheep wandering undisturbed across the track. I feel malice.

They are only at the first gate, barely the start of our routine walk. They are metropolitan weeds. Timothy is leaning gingerly against the lichened granite gatepost, shoe-horning a finger into the arch of his foot. What did he expect wearing daft snakeskin loafers? He mimes clown pain.

Scarlet Barr, fool, is laughing like all this is funny, not knowing she is doomed.

When I have my way, they will get lost. I think with glee of poison adders and bogs that drown up on the moor.

But, damn! They've got us still in earshot. Timothy's voice is piercing to me.

'*Do* slow down, sweethearts,' he is demanding in vulgar city tones that enrage the landscape. Sheep's hooves clatter over crumbled dry-stone walls. Curlews squawk past weather-razed hawthorn stumps.

I pretend I am not hearing.

'Darlings!' he continues in his spoiled voice.

115

I can't believe this. Dad is pandering – not just stopping, but turning. His wide-opened eyes and upturned corners of his mouth are concerned, even *keen*.

Our walk is being interrupted! I glance round desperately, as if the moor horizon or trickling stream can tell me how to spell it out to Dad that they, Scarlet Barr in particular, are our enemies.

I tug my coat sleeves so tight around my waist I might vomit. She is ruining everything. She is not allied now physically with her associates. Tim, standing petulant at the gatepost, is saying he and Roberto can't go on. This should be cause for my sadistic celebration. But their easy defeat is only effective if Scarlet Barr is thoroughly implicated. Against all my expectations and intentions, she is walking upwards, towards us.

She yells down to the people who are supposed to be the friends who would reclaim her, 'We won't be long, promise! We'll only go as far as the second gate.'

Dad looks pleased in a way that makes me feel despair. With my teeth, I rip a piece of skin off down my finger. At least I can predict the stinging blood.

But then, I think, I have worried unnecessarily. Scarlet Barr's steps mince circuitously round sludge-filled ruts. Any minute, she will surely begin her pouting drama queen demands: that we must slow our pace for her.

Dad sets the long-legged striding pace. I run to get in line. I make my back emanate disdain towards where Scarlet Barr must be. I try to make my gait completely enthusiastic. It's hard because a niggling reminds me that normally I'd whine about the regimented walks, all those bleak miles to the Marker. I force myself to think about the way jolly people's legs go walking like they're lifted by balloons. I heave my shoulders to make me lighter.

But what's this? Scarlet Barr's running lightly

past me, carelessly mud-spraying – grabbing hold of Dad's arm! She was supposed to be trailing. And Dad's not supposed to take notice of anything except getting to the Marker and back as ridiculously fast as possible.

I'd like to become a bomb that could explode them into smithereens.

He is responding to Scarlet Barr's arm linked through his by changing his pace to accommodate hers. He has betrayed me, and now Max has too, dodging past my glare and puppying round them.

But perhaps it is by accident of who is closest. Suddenly, I am running as ground-shakingly fast as possible, swerving elaborately round Scarlet Barr as if she is composed of cowpats. I *crash* against the five-bar wooden gate. Directly in front of him, I fix my eyes, burning with hostility, on Dad, to remind him that the reason we have to stop here, only at the second gate, is because of the promise Scarlet Barr made to *her* friends.

His brows close over. I am triumphant! I turn to gloat on Scarlet Barr.

Scarlet Barr looks more disappointed than Dad does that we can't go on. I am undermined. This is entirely out of character. I want to tell her – why inflict these persona modifications on me now?

I charge downhill. I don't care about this bloody walk anyway.

We're nearly home. I delay, in the middle of the road. Max and Phyll are starting to run in excited anticipation of how things are different when Scarlet has guests in the house.

'Of course,' I call out spike-casually, 'I *could* tell you about the school-tie code now.'

Phyll stops. Max, confused, tries to stop as well. His still running legs take him round on the spot. Dad **117** beyond them is just about to shout back some Scarlet Barr related order.

I join Max turning. Max's eyes and mouth are stretching into a revolving blur. I call out at Phyll, breathlessly sadistic, '*Maybe* you have to wear the tie reversed' – spinning faster – 'or *maybe* it's to do with how you tuck it.'

Phyll has to weave and duck and repeat, growling, 'Tell me! *Tell* me!'

My mood wurlitzers into the childishness that is licence for outright rebellion against Dad. I giggle like a spiteful hyena. I allow my wildly swinging hand to hit Max so he goes off course, a crazy spinning top. Dad can't scold me. We have company.

From where he is trying to instruct us something, Dad careers out of his control from one side of my vision to the other. Collapsing in a heap with Max and sticking my tongue out at Phyll, I dizzily pretend I don't, but I know what he's saying. We all do. In my head I mimic sourly, 'Don't forget your wood for the fire. Natural resources.'

Despite Phyll's sparking aggravation, this sort of unites us. Do we comply?

I grab a token twig from the ditch. Phyll and Max do too. Why should *we* be the ones to pick up lots of wood, if the fire happens entirely for Scarlet Barr's benefit?

It's still summer. But she thinks a real fire is *romantic*.

We get the unprecedented treat of not only biscuits – chocolate covered – but also crumpets, gloriously unnutritional, toasted over flames. Every day could be like this . . .

I stop this train of thought. It is despicable city-type behaviour of her to not be satisfied with cooking crumpets properly under the grill.

118   Inside the back door, Phyll and Max and I chuck

our twigs on the red-tiled floor. *Stupid* Sunday teatime, my wrist-flick says.

Ignoring Timothy, Roberto and Scarlet Barr, and especially Dad, I instigate the wellington-removing race. Phyll won't join in with me, but she can't help joining in with Max.

Melted golden butter flooding raspberry jam seeds through the crumpet holes and sealing up the chipped bits of the plate.

We can't lever our toes and heels against the bottom-edge of the coat cupboard fast enough, but the rules of the game dictate: hands can't touch boots. I'm clutching on to Max and coats and hangers, writhing for precarious balance. I'm nearly winning – when, 'Puffballs!'

That infuriating voice is Timothy's. What's he on about now? Only, I can't help conceding him some attention, because he sounds elated. About fungi?

'You have puffballs!' He's pointing out of the window to the back field. 'And one's the size of a football!'

'Oh Roberto,' Timothy says doe-eyed tenderly yet also smirking; he lays his hand on Roberto's arm, 'we can have puffballs for tea.'

There is nothing in the *fact* of puffballs that justifies how Roberto's stony elegance is cracking. I look quickly, harshly, to Scarlet Barr to see if she understands what's really going on.

Scarlet Barr is practically crumpling to the floor with laughing. Surely Phyll can't understand, but she is joining in by smiling. She is even moving closer.

I am above all this frivolity. Although, I would like to know the joke, most of all because Dad's hand is rumpling his hair into a Tintin quiff in a way that indicates he's out of his depth. His brow wrinkles up bemused. I would like to be able to make him feel belittled.

I don't have to.

'Martin!' cries Timothy in mock horror at Dad. 'You have the biggest puffballs in the world and you don't know what to do with them?'

'Ah-hem, no,' Dad confesses gravely.

Scarlet Barr's immaculate eyes are squeezing out hilarity tears.

Over by the back door, suppressing the possibility of fun that's spiralling inside me, I manage to continue looking grim. I have won in some way after all. There is such huge amounts of teasing and it is at Dad's expense.

Of course, this is not to say I side with the weed metropolitans.

Timothy thinks he's clever, I suppose, explaining that the puffball is sliced into bite-sized pieces and fried. Nevertheless I listen intently. It's like a tide of exoticness is swelling in the sparse stone kitchen.

The puffball, it seems, is then eaten on toast with jam or honey. The texture and taste are like fried egg-white.

I revert to my real self.

So, fists aggressive on my hips, I emanate, why bother? Egg-white is tasteless. This is obviously all about the jam, honey and toast. Why not skip the puffball?

But Timothy is rushing past us, outside to get the puffball. Roberto's striding haughtily to join him. And suddenly Max is running too, calling, 'Can I help you, can I help?'

Doing a tiger leap in the grass of the back field, Timothy grabs to tickle Max's stomach. I can't stop myself from feeling jealous. Max might explode with happiness. Timothy winks at Max and pulls him forwards to do a joint rugby tackle on Roberto.

I *stamp* my foot to get me back to here.

They're rolling about like silly little boys.

And yet, the fire's roaring next door and the

pan's spitting on the stove ready to fry. Here has become enticing.

I reject my curiosity about the puffballs. I refuse that there is even the remotest thing to like about Scarlet Barr's friend Timothy.

Sidled near the big square tin that only appears when Scarlet comes, Phyll has seen her chance to slide her hand in and sneak an extra biscuit. I see another opportunity to get at her. Her eye-widening panic gratifyingly lets me know she thinks I'm going to tell. I flatten my lips and shift brows sideways. This is my look of scornful pity. And now I shake my head to more clearly intimate, You think that's naughty? Enjoy your pathetic stolen biscuit while you can. You'll find things *very tough* at Big School.'

■

Without even grabbing a piece of bread from the table for my breakfast, I have to slink outside. The sun burns my face like a truth detector.

It is Phyll's first day setting off for Big School.

I wish I could go back twelve months and change how I behaved. Of *course* I exaggerated Big School. She should know it won't be as bad as I made out. I could have helped her. I wanted her to look up to me. It was stupid and selfish of me. And it didn't even work. We could be nearly getting to be friends.

Instead, through the back-door window, it is Max she is rushing close to for support. Jars of jam and the milk bottle and thick mugs seem to tower to shield my sister and my brother from me. But I am not stopped from seeing them.

Phyll's far-away brown eyes are receptive, no hint of glowering; she tilts nearer Max. Her mime-expression asks him, does she look OK? His head nods so fast it looks ready to fall off. She lets him hold her sleeve.

Does she look OK? She looks *normal*. She looks like she will fit in. The school uniform should be all wonky in proportions on her, the way her shoulders stretch the seams and her legs go on for ever. But she dwarfs the regimented clothes. They don't constrain her.

The window reflects at me that the collar saws my neck. The way I safety-pinned my waistband tighter strangulates my breathing.

I press my forehead, nose and hands up flat against the chilling glass. I'll remind them; I'll destroy their cosiness: I yell, reverberating spite, 'It's gone eight o'clock and Dad's not even up yet!' Max may have Phyll, but he's not got Dad, who's not bothered enough to make sure he gets Phyll to the bus on time for this thing she cares about so massively – her first day at Big School.

Max and Phyll stare at me like I am a condemned person removed from them by bars. Max holds Phyll's sleeve tighter.

■

Ages seem to have gone by of me waiting for things to get back to how they were, at least when Scarlet Barr's not here. But Dad's even more distant.

The scaffolding is still the same. Every dinner-time we each tell about our day at school. We take it in turns to cook; we take it in turns to talk. All completely fair. Like now.

'And then I came home,' I chant mechanically. I plant my head on my hands and my elbows on the table. I haven't stopped wanting but I've given up hoping that Dad will really listen.

Max's voice goes on automatic, 'Today I had French. I learnt *chou-fleur*. Then . . . '

Dad's making a toothpick out of a matchstick.

Something must be stuck, like maybe a bit of bayleaf – and that's more important than Max's day . . .

I stare down at pasta strands worming out from under congealed together globs of mince. Three-quarters finished spaghetti bolognese. It's Max's one dish. I won't appear to enjoy it, because he rejected my assertion that celery *is* a valid bolognese ingredient and he should put it in. Neither him nor Dad seem to care about my authority any more.

Phyll has scraped her plate clean and clatteringly points her knife and fork towards my disobedience. I have to avoid her glare, because it makes my stomach curdle from guilt. Although, as for her thinking she'll get me told off for leaving food, Dad won't even notice. He's remembered something suddenly and is leaning sideways down to take out a file from his briefcase.

Max's voice is pitching up, *demanding* that we listen.

'And then I did ballet. Dawn Crawley kicked my leg during *jetés*.'

Well *of course* she did. No other boys do ballet.

Even still keeping on his mauve T-shirt and orange check-patched cords, when Max eases into place the skin-pink elasticated ballet shoes, he may as well paint himself into white-blue-red circles and set himself up for target practice. But I can't even relish the thought of Max getting into his whine. It will only grate my ears, because it will have no useful effect. Dad merely sees the ballet as a form of exercise. He's missed the key emphasis, that Max was *kicked*.

Dad absent-mindedly scribbles a couple of notes in the file margin. 'Mmm?'

'I have a bruise. I can show it to you,' Max challenges. Dad scratches his ridged brow then gradually begins to focus on his son. It's like he has an internal alarm that clangs when too many sentences have gone by that are void of academic content.

Dad demands, 'And didn't you have a Maths test?' He's looking at Max now – stern. 'How did you do?'

Max revels in the full attention before he says, 'I came bottom of the class.'

'Hmm,' says Dad with a frown. His file is seeming to call his eyes back; his hand clutches tight on to the pencil.

It's not that he doesn't give a damn. I can't believe that. His policy is to not interfere. Max doesn't realise. He's squinting anger. Dad's resigned. 'What next?' he wants to know.

Max clatters his fork angrily. 'Then,' he says, sticking his nose in the air and folding his hands primly in his lap, mimicking me, 'Then I had Geography and Physics.' He simpers. 'Then I came home.' He didn't have Geography or Physics. Will Dad catch him out? Course not. He registers 'came home' and cues Phyll with a nod.

Turns are all very well, but why can't I leave when I've done mine? At least Max directs his aggravation against Dad. Weeks into Big School, and when Phyll tells her day, her glowering eyes *still* attack me. At least she has to initially address Dad.

'First I got up . . . ' she mumbles reluctantly.

I give a bored loud click of my tongue. 'We *all* did *that*!' I mouth. 'Tell us something we *don't* know!'

Dad is intent making file notes.

'Then no-one,' she declares at me, 'flushed anyone's head down the toilet with bleach.'

I do my oh-no-not-*this*-again eyes hooking up to the ceiling look.

'Then,' she goes on, recalling an even tone for Dad's benefit, 'I had games.'

'Then I *scived* games, I'll bet you mean,' I mutter.

Phyll thrashes her hand out at me. 'Then I had . . . '

Max offers with miming of drinking and turning on the tap to get her a glass of water.

Dad's fiddling his toothpick again.

'Then I came home,' states Phyll. She scrapes her chair back loudly and leaves the kitchen, her stiff clenched fists allowing only Max to follow.

■

Phyll and Max can make themselves scarce, upstairs. Lying on my bed in the room off the kitchen, I can block my ears and repeat out loud, 'Can't hear, can't hear, won't hear . . . ' But the thing is that I *know*. I know that the first ring of the telephone has turned Dad to stone at the kitchen table where he's positioned himself with work papers and a bottle of whisky. Maybe she's due to arrive in a couple of hours, or hasn't bothered to ring for days and days.

The second ring of the telephone and he moves fractionally backwards. The third causes an instantaneous widening of the eyes that surprises his glasses off the bridge of his nose. People who don't understand him would blink and miss it. They wouldn't see that this was a well of hurt opened up and sealed over again in a split second.

Sometimes she decides on a whim, which must be barbed subconsciously with spite, not to come after all. He gives her no idea what that does to him.

If I didn't know, I'd stay shut away and carry on with my homework.

By the fourth ring of the telephone I am standing facing my bedroom door. The shakily stuck together planks don't keep out noise; I can see chinks of kitchen clearly through the gaps. I hear the bottle clink the side of the glass as Dad pours himself a fortifying top-up. He takes the glass with him towards the telephone.

As he picks up the receiver, I ease up the latch. **125**

I object to going. I have no choice. He might appreciate my sitting hunched up on the stone steps that lead down from my room.

'Hello,' he barks into the receiver. He removes all possibility of emotion from his voice. He can't entirely control his face. I don't hear what's said to him down the phone by Scarlet Barr, but I see the tiny movements – as if there was momentarily something in his eye that he had to dislodge with two quick blinks. Then immediately he's concentrating on her, on why it's absolutely right that she should stay on at the party and have a good time; that it's even rather good if she doesn't come till tomorrow, that he does have some work he'd not been expecting.

He says all this like he's in a trance.

'See you soon, then,' he pronounces in a matter of fact sort of way. He puts the phone down with authority. But as soon as he hasn't got the receiver to grasp hold of, he's stranded by the coat cupboard, with his whisky glass slipping precariously in his hand.

He thinks saying something will help gather himself together. He addresses the whisky glass: 'Urrm . . . she can't . . . ahhh . . . can't make it over . . . '

His head thrusts forwards. He works his eyebrows. His mouth creaks open, shut again, open.

A reprimand will let out some of the frustration. He rises to his full height, turns and snaps, 'Haven't you got homework to do?'

I don't tell him it's already way past my bedtime. I nod non-committally and make sure to smile. I know that if he actually *saw* the smile properly he'd know it was false, because what I really want to do is shout out frustration.

I don't bother going for the tap on the cheek that serves for a good-night kiss. Even from the other side of the room, his brittleness indicates that any physical contact would cause at best aggravation.

He doesn't even notice if I stay hovering on the steps or walk defiantly past him to go upstairs to the bathroom.

He fills his glass to the brim and wanders pointlessly towards the living-room.

Back inside *my* space I heave and scrape my bed so it barricades shut the thin plank door.

Upstairs in my old room I could see for miles, right across to the opposite green and purple moor. I *don't* miss it. I wanted change. Down here, in *my* room, I seem to be dug in. In front of my ground-floor window there is a trench, that's like a slab stone coffin. It's what stops the back field's black marsh liquid seeping in.

My section of the house is death quiet, Dad and Phyll and Max retired for sleep upstairs. And Mary's dead and I know it's my fault Benjy's gone; and because Leda's still alive, Dad won't get another cat. But the Persian's useless.

I scramble over to my bentwood chair and sit, still, my hands shoved into the shafting anglepoise light that cuts a circle in the centre of my pinewood desk.

Soon the mice will start.

I fill my vision with the cartridge pen and orange fine-ruled exercise book. I wrap my skinny fingers round the plastic casing of the pen, that feels most solid at this moment of anything anywhere. I make a warning thunder-paper sound as I open up the exercise-book diary.

At the top of a pre-lined page I print, in huge, dominating capitals: 'AT SCHOOL'.

At school, I have control. I can ignore Heather Robinson or have her as my friend in class. With Karen Crawley, our mutual convenience is satisfactorily clear-cut. Even Bev Grant does not disturb me.

I cram my mind with Utley comprehensive.

127

Of course, I can't help thinking that Bev Grant's been silly. The pleating's wonky on her tent-like tartan skirt. All that effort with the make-up and it doesn't work. Her face is puffy; tiredness shows behind the foundation. When she walks into the school corridor, every pupil falls silent. Even Paul Cragg.

She only got pregnant for a dare, and it was one she set herself.

Pupils press against the walls to let her past. Someone sneers under their breath, 'Slut.'

I have control. I sneer at her along with everyone, my lip curling below my glasses-hair mask.

My glasses-hair mask. It was supposed to be invincible. I don't want to think how it failed me.

No-one, ever, is supposed to let their stick swing above shoulder level during hockey. Not *ever*.

It was one of the hard girls, headed for goal with the ball.

Thwack – the flat edge of her stick with all her force on the right side of my chest. No amount of glasses coverage could hide my pain, because it was doubling up my body.

I refused to let my hands go near. I reeled and agonied in the frosted mud of the field while the hard girl laughed and carried on. My only regret is that the hard girl did not whack dead them both.

I hate it that my chest is being speared by two steel ballbearings.

The mice are coming out, scuttling round the skirting in the larder, over to the fridge, up behind the stove. I can hear it all.

Dad sets up traps. I *told* him poison, *please* not traps.

I lie in bed and get the stretchy thing. My arm is swelling up so big it's forced to edge up by the three stone steps, where the farmer used to store his live-

stock carcasses, raw red dripping shanks and ribs.

I hear the mechanism of a trap go off. It's supposed to snap their bodies clean in half. It comes down on their nose or paw or tail. They stay alive for hours through the night. The endless death squeal pierces my head, drilling through my consciousness, while I can't move because my legs are filling out to rhomboid or my hands are squeezing into tiny tubes or my stomach's revolving and rising to the ceiling.

It's best to just stay here. Awake. At my desk. The cone of anglepoise contains me.

■

1977

The morning sun hurts my eyes. Its shafts concentrate through the lenses of my glasses, blow-torching my sleep-quavering eyelids.

It seems only yesterday I was starting Big School, tugging nervously at my defensive uniform tie-tongue. Now, the pre-knotted tie looped in my hand ready to lasso over my head feels it will tighten like a noose. It's been two years.

Time goes too fast. I want it to be something I can hold on to, a guiding rope, that I can feed through my hands, at *my* pace. Instead, it whipcracks and a whole section of my life is gone.

The backs of my knees, bare below my fraying navy A-line skirt, I bash against the cold stone bench, as if this millstone grit might be something solid everlasting.

Behind me through the half-closed back door I can hear Max crashing grill and chairs and kettle in the kitchen. The post van is red-glinting up the winding road.

The postman used to arrive in exact time to interrupt our chaos breakfasts, to enjoy a smile at Dad veering absent-mindedly round from the stairwell, sometimes naked except for shoes, underpants and glasses. Then breakfasts changed. It seemed the postman made sure to always turn up late, after we'd grouched and snapped our way to school.

Today, my stomach transforms to lacerating acid as the post van tyre-crunches gravel into our yard, early. I concentrate on pulling up my once-white rumpled socks. His smart blue suit is like civilisation misplaced, marching up the path between the built-up flower-beds that once contained wild strawberries and roses but now are twisting thorns and weeds.

I fiddle hair to be straggly over my glasses. I *yank* at my yellowed polyester shirt-cuffs, not managing to get them down to reach my wrist-bones. The postman's face is awkward. He has his hands stretched out, fingers seeming to bend out of distaste away from the package that he's disclaiming.

I could count each microscopic fibre of the dizzily expanding brown paper, it gets so close before I take it. Black ink snakes across my vision. How long since I've seen it? But I know the handwriting instantly.

'Alison, Phyllis and Maximillian Bennett.'

Who else would write our names in full like that – declaring a fundamental right to do so that is *not* admissable?

Maybe this is reconciliation. But I must be hard. It's simple. She left.

'Eight o'— ' Max must stop his morning waking call. I need time before Dad is got up. I daren't open it alone. Much as I can't admit it, I need support around me now.

I hold the envelope – that is a special, large-rectangle size – like it's some piece of rubbish. I lean round through the back door and curt command at Max, '*Quiet!* Fetch Phyll.'

It does not cross my mind that he would normally refuse till after he's complied. Waiting outside, I resent the grinding weight of this extra authority. I'd like to wail to someone *else* to deal with this intrusion. I feel aggravation that my morning has been interfered with. I score grit into my shoes.

Phyll and Max, with blanked expressions, tiptoe out. They habitually exclude me. I make sure to look bored almost. On Dad's flagstone patio, I hold the envelope up for them to see the writing. I relish the reaction. Phyll's eyes begin to go in shadow. Max looks unsettled by a ray of hope. I am sharp and businesslike, intolerant: 'Come on.'

I want this to be ended.

I lead the way, sprinting fast, towards the biggest, emptiest barn. Slam the massive, creaky doors behind us; secure them shut.

And then there is an awkward pause. Just our three's panic breathing and the package. Particles of ancient, musty hay get up my nose and, agitating, make me violently sneeze them out.

We're jolted into forgetting for a moment that we're enemies.

'Let's open it all at once,' I say. We rip brown paper, and reveal . . .

The back of a card. We stare nonplussed at the glossy white cardboard rectangle.

All my confidence is undermined. Max and Phyll have let go, leaving me in charge of turning right-way-up this object.

My eyes sting from staring at the tasteful reproduction. Quivering stamens and curling petals and stretching stalks of lilies. Is this supposed to be indicating something, like birth or death, or was the choice of artwork arbitrary?

My hands are quivering from fear and expectation. The only way to keep them taut is to pull open this card.

'MARRIED'

The word leaps out and spits at me.

Inside my head, I'm screaming, '*How could you betray us?*'

Confetti swirls round button-hole carnations and our mother standing with a man we do not know, their hands gripped, gold bands glinting sunlight.

I point my finger to the pertinent sentence.

Max looks like he might be turning to hysteria. Phyll's glowered eyes are ominous. The air around is whipping up to boiling hurricane.

'She also says,' I declare abruptly. '"Hope you can share in my happiness."'

This has gone from my control. It's not my fault.

Phyll fists the scribbled cardboard from my hand and wrenches to oblivion. Max whacks the envelope to the dampness of the concrete floor and jumps and stamps it into pulp.

The pounding of my head won't stop. With my fingers pressing pain into my forehead, I tally up the facts.

She is married. She made an error in deciding to inform us. The evidence has been destroyed.

Cowering begind the final dry-stone wall, draggled sheep stare at me as if I am a lunatic.

And fuck you too.

I want peace. It suddenly – crazily – seems I have seen where to find it.

In late afternoon, when it is not safe to start out, I am climbing fast towards Birch Wood. From where I am scrambling up the track, it looks ethereal, with soft pink and silver glinting the bark of the trees, which reach up spindly, their branches linking into a sheltering umbrella that stretches parallel with the heavens.

133

My mind will be eliminated by blasting ice wind. I will merge benighted into feelingless bark.

I concentrate on the irritating, uneven ground that I have to negotiate to get there. I slip on trickling mud; grasp hold of reeds to yank me up.

But now I am here, in the wood, I look around me, desolated. The birch umbrella has disintegrated. Stick branches stab at the cold white sky.

1978

How can it be clear blue with blazing sunshine then blacked-out hail clouds when it's only seconds later that I glance, yearning, out the shop window over the grime roofs of Utley town?

I have two pairs of socks on. It is not enough. My toes are separating out like they have been freeze-thawed. Stupid flimsy *fashion item* shoes. They are punishing me for irresolution.

Bent again behind the formica counter, I tumble mud-cased potatoes with extra crashing determination. They thunder from the hip-height layered-paper sack into green plastic display cases lined up on the concrete floor.

This earns me money. It is sociable. Everyone at Utley School at one time or another has to get a Saturday job at Mr Cheap Potato's.

Mr Wiggly saw me through the window last week. He took me aside after the Maths lesson to express his concern. I'm a bright girl, he said, who could do well, and I should beware of letting my studies slip. Exams are coming up.

Dad went *on* about that too. Not for as long as I thought he ought to, though.

So what? It's only one day. I have new expenses to account for. These two-inch platforms, for example. And tartan strips to stick on to my bag.

Karen Crawley arranged the job here for me.

It's all right. I do the bits that no-one else likes. In the vegetable-stacked back-room I do stock accounting; or I lug emptied beet and carrot and celery crates outside. Sometimes I'd like to crawl into a dry soil-lined box and seal it over.

In the front of the shop, Karen Crawley holds court. She is the shop assistant who always steps forward when there's a staff–customer dispute about final totals. She's Queen of the Till. I am some kind of scrappy handmaiden.

I go back to hauling and scrabbling sacks and wood crates about, suddenly objecting to the bowing and scraping that is part of my job.

The erratic dring-dringling of the old-fashioned bell that hangs by string off the shop door corner means more custom, more work. At least it keeps all the counter girls busy. So what's Karen Crawley doing by my side?

As I stand to full height, I *yank* up my knee-high socks, to remind her that I *didn't* get fudge-tint nylons as well, just the stack shoes to compromise.

Karen's not bothered about my legwear rebellion. I'm promoted precariously to Maid of Honour. She's hissing in my ear.

'Ere, look 'oo it is – tha' slut Bev Grant.' Karen's voice gets louder. She's not addressing only me now, but *all* her shop girl minions.

'I always knew she was common, jus' by 'er name: Bev. Up t'spout *again*. Dun't even know t'father. Common as muck. And warr'a mess! Won't yer jus' look arr'er.'

I am looking at her. Everyone in the shop is looking at her. There's dead silence now – not even the chinking of money or the ringing of the till. All the customers and all the staff are staring aggressively at Bev Grant.

She has let herself go. Karen's right. Her hair is lank. Her face is grey and drawn. Smoke streaming up from the cigarette in her mouth makes her screw up her eyes. Her synthetic sweater is shapeless and soiled, punched out by her pregnant stomach.

Why won't she defend herself? Obscured at the back of the shop, I shuffle my stack heels awkwardly.

A couple of girls push Karen forward: "'Ere, *you* serve 'er, go on.'

Bev asks for a pound of Reds and a pound of Golden Delicious. Her voice is tired. Karen purses her lips. She won't look Bev in the eyes. Karen wrinkles her nose as if there's a bad smell in the air. She can't weigh up the apples and potatoes fast enough. She is being overtly rude, but the manager won't object because he'd be glad if Bev Grant never set foot in his establishment again.

Bev Grant's bastard infant outside in the pram begins to cry.

She was so *definite* she would have it adopted. What stopped her? Bev Grant, who could have knuckle-dusted anyone without a twinge of sympathy. She must have cared, loved her child so much, no matter what, she couldn't give it up. I feel bereft.

I have a self-destructive urge to warn her that the Golden Delicious are out of date and soggy.

Without energy or purpose, Bev Grant packs the potatoes and apples into her string bag. Everyone's breath is held, waiting for her to get out.

I hate Bev suddenly. She had control! Standing in the dinner hall when she announced her plan – pregnancy; adoption – she was *hard*. Now her breasts **137** are huge and sagged. How did she get it so completely wrong? And it couldn't have been more public.

The tension in the shop's unbearable. Bev Grant moves towards the door. Her walk's slowed to a shuffle. One hand's stuck, wearily supporting, in her back.

Outside, Bev begins to creak her pram towards the other side of town. I can't see her any more. Customers and shop-girls have swarmed the streetfront window. Sneering faces ogle round the painted on shop name, which from here is backwards:

OTATOP ЧАƎHƆ ЯM

It's like it's indicating everything it frames is nonsense. But it's not. It's indelible as if it's branded on her. Bev Grant's a slut.

She was only trying to work things out.

■

Phyll, Max and I are not really old enough to wreck the house, but we can get people in who are. News travels fast at school. 'The Bennetts' Dad's away.' Chinese whispers down the corridor; details scribbled on cigarette packets and passed around behind the bike sheds; older brothers and sisters phoned up at work; and between Friday afternoon and Saturday evening, a battalion of borrowed tractors, vans and bashed-up minis is assembled ready to ascend the tarmac strip marked 'High Kirkby – No Through Road.'

It's the perfect party venue, our house: right out on the edge of the moor. No neighbours to annoy. Father who doesn't care. Or at least, that's what he says.

'Do what you like, but no-one sleeps in my bed.' This is his one rule. Nine, ten, twelve people end up in there, under his aubergine snowflake patterned cover, smoking and necking; boys seeing how far they can go how fast, girls struggling to twang their bra straps back into place.

Dad minds a lot. He's given up – on the house, and on us. An accidental brush of shoulders on the stairs can spark screaming, kicking rages that take plaster off the walls, chairs to splinters, doors off their hinges.

Mrs Taylor says we've changed. She purses her lips before hurling her whole energy into clenching the rag she's using to clean the window. She's known us since we were born. There's not much can upset her.

She might even cry if she knew I'd let boys tie bangers to Leda's tail. Singed white fur was the last I saw of her.

If it's the Monday after one of the accidental parties, Mrs Taylor doesn't comment on the used condoms at the back of the larder, or the lentils poured in the soap compartment of the washing-machine. She doesn't say anything at all. When we've got back from school, she carries on with her cleaning routine until Dad's car crunches into the drive. She'll hardly touch our rooms anymore.

Max's has his chess-board and ballet outfit trashed in one corner to leave more space for shelves to hold aloft his hi-fi. He stares at the plaster that dribbled from the mis-drilled holes in the wall forming neat piles on the floorboards. Headphones slice into his mohican. He taps time with chewed fingernail on mud-encrusted army trousers in time to the aggression of The Damned.

In Phyll's room, the shaky louvre door and ply-wood wardrobe, that Dad built, is axed to open plan. Around the floor is dotted empty cans of beer and ashtrays over-piled with ground-out cigarettes. Mine's not much changed, except the desk has practically become an armoury: cosmetics; styling products.

Hair laquer, Karen Crawley nagged at me, use hair laquer and flick it back. 'Yer fringe meks yer look *immature*,' she said. So I got rid of the fringe – by cutting the rest the same length. Bowl-shaped, turned *under*. If I am to be her gutless acolyte, I will at least subvert.

It is usual in terms of make-up to wear charcoal or brown eyeliner, kohled thick beneath the eye. I wear a blue that turns luminously turquoise as it dissolves gradually through the day and seeps down my cheeks, almost like a wash of tears, except my eyes behind the glasses I stubbornly keep on are hard.

I dress like this for school, and I wear the same for my parties. Karen Crawley comes up from her house early. She says it's to help me get ready, in order that I don't embarrass myself.

Her mother hasn't realised about the exhaust spewing, honking vehicles that race past her house, spraying crushed beer cans and fag ends at her garden, at the Pillar, at the curious cows snorting towards the steep, winding road. Mrs Crawley doesn't know 'them louts' come here. She thinks a night at the Bennetts will be civilising for her Karen.

Karen spends fifty-five minutes in the bathroom applying extra laquer on her hair. Another layer of mascara. Another swipe of rust blusher.

I spend that time stacking furniture against my bedroom door. One thing I won't do is snog some school-boy in my bed. *No-one* comes in my room. I barricade the door and climb out the window, over the slab-stone trench, into the back field. I go round, dodging nettles and gorse, and I come in, ready for my party, like everyone else, through the back door.

I wheel Dad's swivel chair over to the window and, twirling the seat occasionally for dizziness in bored anticipation of sticky lager and cider, and Pernod and black, I watch and listen for the invasion.

It depends which way the wind's blowing whether

I hear engines forced growling up the 1 in 10 gradient first or see headlights fighting to be fastest over the brow of the hill. Some drivers achieve several inches air space between tyre and tarmac.

The yard clouds with dust as the first few cars screech into the gravel; vans and tractors churn parking-space out of the front field. Disgruntled delegates are shoved roughly out of car doors with yelled instructions to race and stake their gang's claim on the record player – mono, with a creaky plastic arm mechanism for dropping down singles. A girl with tartan pleated midi-skirt and flicked back straw hair elbows out of the way a boy with skin-tight black drainpipes and coal cockatoo tuft so she can get first up the flagstone path with her Bay City Roller numbers. The boy's winkle-pickers are nearly as feet-shackling as the girl's seven-inch platforms, but he sussed out a short cut: skip the path between raised flower-beds that lead to the back door. The coal cockatoo tuft diverts into the front garden and through the front door: a direct route to the 'sound system'. Cockatoo tuft drooping slightly from perspiration but face and stance triumphant, he rushes to stack on the turntable's chrome stalk, skull and cross bone logo-ed Dead Kennedys.

I don't move from Dad's swivel chair, staring out the window as our house fills with irate squealing guitar solos and gangs of girls and gangs of boys performing the preliminaries for coupling off into necking sessions.

First, they ignore each other. There are heroics and provocations – competitions between boys for drinking Special Brew in precarious positions; giggling from girls who try and push them over.

Phyll leads a guerrilla group on a mission to do specific domestic damage. It perplexes and isolates me further that she looks like she might be having fun. Like the lentils in the washing-machine was her idea, and chipping off the top edge of the crockery bread-bin so it fitted in the oven to see if it was heat proof. Max sometimes doesn't come down at all. Scrunched in the corner by his own private hi-fi, he turns up the volume and clamps the squidgy black plastic padding of his headphones tighter to his ears. He doesn't even look round when the first couples start peering in to see if his bed's free. He simply puts on a louder record when there's one couple experimenting in his bed and one going for all out copulation behind him on the floor.

I stay in the corner of the dining-room, in Dad's swivel chair, staring at the reflections in the blackened window. I can stay there for about two hours while Karen does flirtatious giggling with the gang of girls headed by the one bearing Bay City Rollers' singles. I see when Karen has decided who she fancies because the giggling suddenly stops. She takes out a special lip-stick holder and touches the peach-succulent lip-gloss shine on her thin lips. Then she glares impatiently at my back. I see all this mirrored, shimmering flat over the night-time landscape. I sigh boredom and rise to join her. She has already been doing eye signals with her chosen partner, so it doesn't take long for me to be pushed off into a corner with his mate.

I do all the things that are proper on these occasions. I drink snakebites until I throw up, as naturally as coughing, averting my head so it misses my clothes. But I don't have conversation with my partner. I won't allow him to touch me until we have climbed the stairs and reached the guest bed. If others are in there, I stand staring, condensing distaste and above-it-all impassiveness, until they become embarrassed, scramble back into their clothes and leave, maybe for Dad's bed, maybe for one of the barns.

This was Scarlet's workspace. This was where mum slept when she had screamed herself hoarse at

Dad's perplexed, angry shouting.

There is only a certain amount I will allow. I remove my glasses and hold tight on to them for safe-keeping. The boy in question may wiggle his tongue in my mouth. He feels triumph; I feel scorn. Is he too drunk to notice or too desperate to care about how I taste of vomit? He can fumble up the back of my shirt, groping for a bra strap that I won't wear. His confused pause is all I need to appear to remember myself. He renews his fumblings; I refuse, with a physical will that surprises his tongue out of my mouth.

Ice-maiden. Frigid. I know those taunts will come. But for now it is acceptable – they think I am 'a nice girl' to refuse.

Intense boredom, and the fact that my head is spinning dangerously, cause me to lean back into the corner and slowly close my eyes. I wait for the releasing sound of the boy shutting the door.

I have done my duty. In a drunk nausea haze I conclude that it is time to return to my room. I turn to check that the guest-room is wrecked.

Downstairs and through the dining-room, I nego-tiate necking couples and comatose teenagers. By the time I reach the back door I am feeling ready to collapse groaning on the floor. I think fresh air will help, but the blood merely spins faster inside my head. I sway against the door jamb, sink into the edge of the stone bench, arms spread out over it for support. My stomach twists acid-juiced nausea up into my throat. My eyes are parched.

And then I feel a hand, firm, holding me steady at my waist. The other hand rubs my back. Soothing away the strain. And I remain completely still, not daring to move in case it stops. I know who it is without turning round. I know I should acknowledge the help. But then I would reject it.

Flatten my face on to the cold stone bench; wrap my arms into a layer of protection over my head, and **143** feel the hand on my back creating spreading dizzying warmth.

Sunday

Last night Paul Cragg helped me back to my room. He didn't stay.

My hands and bespectacled face are trapped in the yellow cone of anglepoise light; outside, the blackness of nettles and gorse silhouetted against deeper blackness stretch into the emptiness of the moor.

He didn't stay. I didn't ask him. I wouldn't have let him.

The pointlessness of writing things down is overwhelming.

■

1979

I don't give a damn that this is his only private space. I will eat my dinner in Dad's bedroom. Why should he be bothered? He's never here.

Crouch down on the end of the snowflake-patterned cover of his bed.

And what kind of dinner is it anyway: disgusting. Boiled rice and fortnight-old fried cabbage, because there's nothing else. Not from shopping. That routine has ended. The vegetable patch is seeded over.

On the larder middle shelf, at the murky back, glued in by droppings, I found one condiment. A bottle of Lea & Perrins sauce, cement-caked in dust. It doesn't make the bile food more palatable. It only changes its disgustingness. It savages my tongue so that the mush must be spat out or salivated quick down like poison.

Still three-quarters of it left, and I have no hunger. I push it round the plate with my fork.

'*Don't* play with your food!' he'd say. I can mimic him exactly, with his lashed brow and grinding jaw, **145** but instead I choose to contort my face into whining sneering that would infuriate him.

Playing with one's food – that sounds like FUN. Greyed grains of rice slime between my two fingertips. With a gay flick of my wrist, I sprinkle them on Dad's bedspread, as one might scatter seasoning upon a platter of delectables. I grind my dinner into his wool cover with the heel of my hand.

The top two handles of his huge, carved chest of drawers are shadowed, staring. I'd like to turn them out, tip his accidentally dyed pink Y-fronts and rolled-up worn-out socks on to the floor. That'd make it easy for him to find the change of underwear he's always packing in his briefcase when he leaves.

Meetings. Conferences.

He has pillow, blanket, toothbrush in his office.

'Sort things out, will you Allie,' he states, his eyes blank. The back door slams behind him before I can hurl abuse.

Sort things out. As if I can *force* Phyll to walk the mile and a half to the school bus.

Maintain the cleaning rota. Me stood in the middle of the kitchen red-tiled floor, knuckles white on mop handle, impotent with rage at Max and Phyll who are determinedly immobile, jibing, '*You're* the one who's bothered. Why should we do it? Clean the house yourself.' Hurl the mop down. Storm off. Block my ears to their hyena laughing.

That's why everything's a mess, and me, reflected in the blackened window. I jerk my head back. Tear-clogged hair stays straggled on my cheek.

The plate, lumped with disintegrating grey, looks stupid on my lap, balanced with distaste as if it's something rotting.

Behind me Dad's plank door is snatched by vagrant wind. The screeching rusted metal of its hinges echoes loud around the empty house.

I have equal rights as anyone to be in this room, the *guest*-room. It's not Scarlet Barr's study any more.

Of course she's left her clickety-clack ancient typewriter here on the side-table. Why would an *actress* have a typewriter anyway? Ostentatious affectation; to stake her claim. But the gun-metal blue cover is being voided by a placid settling of dust.

I put down my pile of homework insolently where her actor notes would be, beside the ghost typewriter. I clatter the chair forwards and sit.

I am faced with Physics, Economics, Maths. The papers layering precariously upwards are wafer-thin square pancakes oozing boringness as distinct to me as syrup.

I gather my Biros and pencils and subject colour-coding felt-tip pens all together in my hand and I drop them on top of the paper pile in spillikins clutter. Distraction tactics, but who is there to care? I look around to see if Scarlet Barr's left any bits and pieces I could add. Nothing on the musty striped cheesecloth cover; not even in the tatty waste-bin at my feet.

But beside the bin is an empty cigarette packet. This is offensive to me for all sorts of reasons I can't immediately get clear. There's the pretentiousness that it contained *menthol* brand. And the pack must have been cast down by one of *Scarlet's* guests.

Barbie, I'll bet it was, with her shelf-like bottom lip drawling square down for an aren't-I-*won*-derful smile.

When she came, she wanted to go to the 'country fête.' *Country fête!* She meant the Skipwith Show.

By then it had become a sort of game, sending the invaders packing. It was too childishly simple.

At the Skipwith Show, I guided her to Nelson, the one-eyed piebald horse, 10p a ride, an ambling ancient. 'What fun!' she cried, gaily confident of sloth. A filly was

147

directed into Nelson's range. The one remaining eye went on the filly, and he was off, a piebald that never trots, now going at full pelt gallop, roller-coasting up the field.

Credit where it's due. With no saddle or reins, and just a mangy mane to grip to, Barbie managed to stay clinging. And I don't think it was she who vowed never to come back, but Scarlet who finally ceased the invitations.

Are we meant to feel *sorry* or something? It's not *our* fault if she takes it personally.

'Martin, Martin,' I overheard her wailing in actress histrionics. 'Do they think I'm made of stone?' She knows this house can be an echo chamber. 'Do they think I have no feelings?'

I come into Max's room because I'm positive he wouldn't like it.

His floor is like a battlefield, littered with failure trophies marking past campaigns. A broken toy doll action man. One shredded ballet-shoe.

And then there was his *stupid* chess obsession.

Evening games and weekend matches, he attended and attended until he'd climbed the under-12's chess league. He got his picture in the local paper.

'Brainy Bennett,' the news-photo caption says. He's nailed it there, bold black and white, in the middle above his ransacked chest of drawers, displayed for Dad to see. It is spite instead that I am standing staring.

Max hasn't got friends. Why is he not here?

My stomach belongs to someone else, who is in contorting, wrenching pain. I will not own it.

Wait for it to pass. Crouch right down. Drive my toes deep into the mattress.

It's gone; only a dull ache left.

I want Phyll to be here. So I can ask her if she has this thing as well. I might cling to her. Her night-shrouded bed sticks out empty in the room.

This one I am on, it used to be *my* bed. I want more than anything now to feel the right to climb inside. There's no blankets, no pillows, no lying space. What was my child's place is subsumed by the equipment of Phyll's change.

Annoyingly, I feel petulant instead of vindictive as I flick the empty bleach bottle with my finger.

So what if she's got crinkly ended hair, gone white from bleach then green from food dye? It doesn't make her *hard*.

I'll bet she doesn't get this twisting agony.

She still had to ask for my help to get her out of a playground fight. 'Allie, please don't let Linda Smith smash my head in.' Phyll's face was soft and pleading right enough when she came with that request. I felt proud and strong. It was like being back at Skipwith, my talking powers invincible.

The pain, it is returning – I can control it, make it cease.

The fight was cancelled due to me. Where was gratitude? Phyll went back to circumnavigating endless corridors and concrete quads in order to avoid me, her prissy elder sister.

Prissy but grown-up, if what I think is right and this is the Period that's happening to me.

And anyway, I wouldn't be seen dead with someone who resorts to such base clothes tactics. Phyll, always brandishing her fold-up scissors to cut *more* strips out of her tartan blue-grey trousers ... What is the point? Dad doesn't notice; teachers aren't bothered because she hasn't even broken any rules.

I resent being in my hunched position here in the **149**

corner of what used to be my bedroom as well as Phyll's.

The hessian curtains that made the morning send through ruby warming light are ripped down.

The window, filled with dark, is unnerving me. I am cold.

Keep my legs clamped *tight* shut. Won't let blood flow. Won't allow it to take up my attention.

Look around, squinting to make out magenta trumpet carpet flowers.

What is these other friends' appeal? She stays out nearly always with them now.

I should go back downstairs, to *my* bedroom, which I have fortified. Except against the mice.

THIS BLOODY AWFUL PAIN!

In my room there is my *diary*. And the mickey mice; cuddly mice – I can believe them nonsense creatures in the day. At night their multiplying scratchy feet, scaling the stone steps from the kitchen to my room, makes my stomach turn to acid.

They're tiny furry things, I know, with beady eyes and cutesy ears. They claw up bedclothes, gnawing on my legs.

I thought I could make myself have control.

Under the anglepoise spotlight my precisely neutered handwriting, that I thought I had made strong, looks absurd, a caricature of itself. I write with a *fountain pen*, but it's a cheap chunky-grip; what I chose for my diary is an orange fine-ruled child's exercise book. The chimes of *News at Ten* can still, even without my realising, start off that stretchy thing – the panic that it's gone ten and I ought to be asleep.

My voice hammers in a closed-off throat that won't allow my screaming.

I thought by now I would be adult.

My boots ring out on tarmac as I pass the rusted sign that says 'High Kirkby – No Through Road'. It is a fine spring day. I pull my military grey overcoat tighter and march up the hill.

Dad is going to sell the house. I may not live there anymore, but I would like to have been consulted.

'Bring a knapsack,' trilled Scarlet Barr over the phone – as if there was no question that all the childhood possessions I wanted to keep would fit in one bag; as if I would take what *she* says as a command when she's only back because we are gone. And I have to come *early*, to help organise and placate Phyll and Max, I suppose. Me, always bloody me.

I secure my glasses to my nose.

I look out over spreading fields of emerald glittering grass. Black-faced lambs kick their heels. A curlew calls from far away in the cornflower sky.

This is even more beautiful than I remembered. It is a mistake for Dad to leave. It's clear to me that Scarlet Barr has somehow made him.

Sturdy dry-stone walls trammel me higher.

If I close my eyes, I can almost see Phyll chucking   **153** her doll's limbs into the raised flower-bed's rose-bushes. There, coming out the back door is punk Max, or chess-playing Max; over in the vegetable patch Dad's digging wormy carrots up for dinner.

Three years' absence is a lifetime and nothing at all. I was here yesterday.

I hold my breath in anticipation as I step over the brow of the hill. A scudding grey cloud obliterates the sun.

Withensty's is falling apart.

Below the bleak moor, my square granite fortress is disintegrating. Roof tiles have crashed past curtain-less windows to the ground. The yard gate is hanging off its hinges. Sleet and hail have scoured away where Max scratched 'Withensty's' crudely with his pen-knife into the gatepost.

My feet strike over thinned-out gravel. The crumbling surrounding dry-stone garden wall in front of me seems sturdier than the house, which has tumbled its contents on to the yellowed, hopelessly uneven lawn.

At the bottom, by the lilac tree, a hacked-up bunk-bed has been piled triangular. An empty pack of firelighters is tossed aside. Infant flames are creeping up, playing round chipped building-blocks, old files of Dad's, the louvre doors off mine and Phyll's wardrobe, and there, a black wool beret, and striped multi-coloured leg-warmers, which belonged to Scarlet Barr. She steps into view. She tosses on top of books and rubbish and clothes, a twirling feather boa.

This belonged to my mother. Scarlet Barr has no right to burn it.

She spots me over the paint-flaking garden gate. 'Allie,' she commands, 'come in!'

I will delay, assessing coolly.

Everything about her always was an exclamation.

Who else would wear chrome-plated half glasses and a

crisp white dress-shirt to build a bonfire? And, of course, the tastefully ragged scarf tied to keep her hair back just happens to perfectly complement her neat hazel eyes.

She can't unsettle me. She may appear to be presiding, but it's my house more than hers.

Our purpose at this moment is to burn. I turn my hostile glare towards the fire and march through the creaking garden gate.

I am standing, bullishly self-contained, in front of an open-air incinerator. Scarlet Barr is somewhere in the unimportant background. Flames sear my face. In the chill spring air, rising heat warps everything around – the black moor opposite dissolves; the wind-twisted lilac tree becomes magnificent. Crocuses shimmer up the moss-green wall, parallel with Scarlet Barr, who has come to stand beside me.

I want to still feel strident.

The pyre is hypnotic. Its crackling is like laughter. Scarlet turns to pick up fuel. It seems that I must too. Scarlet Barr is so close – our shoulders, hands, hair, brush together as we lean and bend, in unison. The fire is more powerful than either of us, drawing us together to meet the demand for more, *more* of the detritus that's tumbling out from the house behind us.

Watch orange tongues of heat caress a bentwood chair that had been smashed against the kitchen wall. A primary-coloured up-across-down drawn house, with 'For Mummy' laboriously scrawled up the side, turns instantly to ash. Feed the fire a bird-shit-splattered sequin skull-cap; enveloping, blistering violet flames reflect themselves.

Scarlet Barr begins to talk, in a confiding tone. Her voice is directed towards the fire, where the skull-cap is being finally devoured.

'In many ways,' she announces quietly, 'I admire your mother.'

This absent-minded choice of subject matter is a

surprise like a block of ice has been smashed into my face. Except, the way Scarlet Barr is talking, I could be one of her dearest friends. She continues in a distant monologue.

'Ten or fifteen years ago, it was inconceivable that a mother should leave her children.'

I am disoriented by the pungent smoke, trying to concentrate.

'Your mother's action could be interpreted as pioneering, feminist even.'

This seems pre-rehearsed, a rationalisation that I wish had stayed inside her head.

'It might be said that she acted with unusual courage.'

The soft movements of Scarlet Barr's mouth are stripped of the familiar stretching, pouting drama. I am staring full at her now. It's as if I've caught her naked. No longer made taut by effortfully arched eyebrows, her eyes are edged with subtle, fanning lines.

She pulls herself sharply together – although not quite enough to look around and remember that she's talking to the subject-matter's daughter.

'Of course, she clearly went quite bonkers.'

Wearing her matter-of-fact mouth-set, Scarlet stokes the fire with a black-and-white photograph of a woman in a 1970s' batik shift-dress. The woman's narrowed eyes are shaded by a hand that seems poised to lash out at the photographer.

'Apparently . . . '

Scarlet, her white face still focused on the roaring flames, has leaned unexpectedly forwards. She is conspiratorial.

'Mrs Taylor can remember the day your mother could no longer bear the sight of you.'

My guts have been turned out on to the ground. They are palpitating, livid vermilion in the dirt.

I can picture Scarlet Barr and Mrs Taylor at the

kitchen table over tea – half a cup, weak, no sugar – Scarlet, desperately curious for the bits of jigsaw she couldn't get from Dad.

I want to smash Scarlet Barr's face in, while I compose myself.

Why wouldn't Mrs Taylor tell *me*?

But then, I know now, so what's the difference.

I suppose Scarlet senses an adverse response. She turns to face me. Her expression tries to make light.

'But really, can you blame her? You must have been terrors.'

Three infants squawling across the red-tiled kitchen floor towards a screaming woman who is wrapped in chains.

I force a pacifying grimace in Scarlet Barr's direction. It is hardly necessary. The crackling, raging fire has had an overpowering effect. Scarlet Barr is locked again into confessional.

'There are certain things your father is unable to face.'

She scatters a handful of photos thoughtfully into the inferno. A picture of a couple, classic 1960s, he in black roll-neck, she in turtle-neck and ski-pants, both ecstatic smiling; their three young children, naked on a Mexican rug, in an idyllic garden setting.

'This caused difficulties.'

The children's eyes are the same as their mother's: large, probing, too expressive for other people's comfort.

With a charring chair-leg, I push my old radiation-green flowered dress deep into the red-hot centre. I thought I'd learnt imperviousness. I had made it my spiteful habit to emanate *hate you – go away – hate you* to Scarlet as a matter of course.

'It became almost impossible for me to maintain a dialogue with your father.'

Dialogue.

This word skips around in my head singing *I'm not what I seem.*

Dad and Scarlet Barr broke up? Might break up?

I am a child who thought I'd had control of stacking up the building blocks, only to find the rock-hard surface I'd been leaned against has got up and walked away.

Without Scarlet Barr I don't know what Dad would have done.

All those years of claw-barring into every fissure, wedging, trying to lever them apart. I'd convinced myself she didn't care.

Suddenly I'm anxious to make up. I hurl into the furnace evidence of my most bolshy teenage years: destructively empty exam papers; a trashed Shakespeare volume; Woolworths' blue eyeshadow I bought with Karen Crawley for some drunken, wrecking party.

The wind conspires to whip up the blaze. I am humiliated by my small-mindedness. I can't look Scarlet in the eye.

Dad shunts the overloaded wheelbarrow across the yard gravel towards us. He is in his foulest, most irritable mood. I want to run up and hammer with my fists, to *make* him cheer up, to yell:

Don't you know how tough she's had to be? Don't you realise you could lose her?

His jaw's grinding. His knuckles on the rusted barrow handles are stretched transparent.

Hunched brittle over his burden, he explodes at Scarlet. 'What the hell am I supposed to do with all this crap?'

The 'crap' is more of Mum's stuff from the barns. Scarlet flashes intense irritation. It is clear they have discussed this already, a great deal. Scarlet is just about to snap at him or storm off. I burst in.

158   'Burn it, Dad.'

Scarlet turns to scour me with her hazel eyes, the fine brows arching over in surprise. Am I, after all, her ally?

With Dad still gripping it, I yank the barrow and upturn the contents.

Tumbling on to the fire, maternity-wear and records and bundled-up letters dislodge the brown singeing photograph of my mother when she was a raw, ambitious young woman trapped in a claustrophobic marriage. The rising batik dress, the lashing, swirling hand demand attention. Dad and Scarlet Barr are intent as well, transfixed beside me. Manacle loops of curling smoke disperse. The photo, flaming green and indigo and turquoise, flies free, up into the sky. It becomes a speck, dancing into blue.

The knapsack I brought with me remains empty at my feet. I don't want to take anything. I skim the mountainous debris behind me. Half hidden by the blue tin train is the orange fine-ruled exercise book that became my diary. Here I tried to confine my life in pre-ruled lines. I almost succeeded in eliminating emotion.

I take this diary, and the empty grey canvas knapsack, and I place them on the fire.

I turn and say to Scarlet Barr, 'If there is anything left of mine, please feel free to burn it.'

Stumbling away from the house, I heave air into my lungs, send clods of earth spraying clumsy all around me, trip and skid and keep on going.

At the brow of the hill, I leap and twist on to the wall. I wedge my feet in between two lumps of millstone grit. I grip my hands on to the rough, cold stone.

Withensty's is fluid in the raging fire's rising heat.

It has no hold on me now.

I swing my legs over the wall, squeeze my eyes **159**

shut and grin like a gleeful mad escaping child as I turn my back on Withensty's. I hurl myself to the ground on the other side, ready to run and run and run.

Only, I am obstructed. I rear back into the wall to see Paul Cragg – always in the wrong place at the wrong time! Smirking like I'll be pleased to see him. Well, he should just get out of my way.

Concentrate aggravation into the set of my jaw and the flash of my eyes. Ducking under his arm, I step sideways; stamp forwards as fast as I can without looking like I'm running away from him.

Except then something makes me turn around. The cheekiness of him, I suppose. The arrogance of thinking he knows me.

His easy pace keeps him a polite two steps behind me. His eyes are laughing down at me.

I am outraged.

I will not take the bait.

'How are you?' I enquire. I don't expect an answer.

I resume my march, slowed to a speed that instructs him to draw alongside me.

His head is bowed, possibly in thought – although that is not my business. Furthermore, I do not care.

I assess him coldly. I may as well since I've no choice but to spend the time of the walk in his company.

The breeze is soothing. The grass is soft beneath my feet.

Paul Cragg has been around as long as I can remember, always unsettling, even when he spent all his time fiddling with those stupid fishing-flies and wire-loop traps. He is everything I am not. He is at ease. He doesn't have to think five million times before he will commit himself to doing something.

He has turned out as handsome as the compre-
160 hensive teachers' sideways glances had suggested. Not

conventional – his features are too extreme: his straw hair's too wild to ever have quiffed up fashionably; his full mouth's too expressive; and his eyes . . .

I am rather thankful that they are for the moment directed at his feet. It is hard to be resolved when he stares right at me.

His gentle voice wraps round me, asking how I am.

Damn him for his sincerity.

Loud-speakered into my brain is the reality.

A Leeds bedsit that has no buzzer because what's the need? No-one calls. And why get the gas fire re-connected when I can save money by wearing my overcoat during evenings of economising lentil stew suppers, which are quite nourishing enough to sustain me in my supremely sensible job? Stack up trays of senior employees' tea; nod courteously when I am loaded down with papers that need distributing in pigeon-holes that are ticker-tape-labelled with everybody's name but mine. Next year, I may be awarded my own desk.

I yank my coat collar hard around my throat, and spit out, 'I'm fine.'

We have come to a stream, which is a convenient distraction. Paul Cragg strides simply over. I don't have the leg span; my energy has been drained. Paul Cragg reaches his arms across to help me.

I have pride! I would rather walk out of my way to a feasible crossing point. I glance haughtily upstream.

The crystal waters are chuckling, chasing through the reeds, somersaulting over black velvet rocks. Except for a cave under the far bank. There the water has eroded into the stone its own gaol, where it is stagnating.

I grasp Paul Cragg's hands. I murmur to myself to ignore the possibility that he might not take my weight.

161

I will look him in the eye. I leap. His blue irises are laughing at me, again! I will teach him – I veer from landing in his arms. I misjudge my footing.

The hard earth is searing at a diagonal across my line of vision. My mind insists I squash my glasses secure on to my face. I have hit horizontal, staring shocked at a distant bobbing white cloud. I can't contemplate how it is that I don't yet feel the bruises.

Paul Cragg has himself hurled practically beneath me. One hand cradles my head; the other is circling my waist.

He begins to breathe again. I do not. Warm air caresses the back of my neck, the down on the side of my cheek.

The scent of crushed wild primroses is intoxicating.

I am collapsing inwards.

This is surely not acceptable.

■

It is glaring daylight outside. I get none in this bedsit room.

That's why I chose it: at the back, with the window opening on to a black brick wall. It's better that way.

The sun burns. It changes people's moods. Things get out of perspective.

The dark is certain. At night when my body starts the stretching, shrinking, twisting – the door that's posted with fire-regulations is locked. Like now, against the phone ringing, far away, a mocking *drrring—drring* in the empty hallway.

It is 11 a.m., Saturday. A bent and broken spring is *jabbing* where I sit on the edge of my single bed. Lit by the dust-iced bare bulb, my hands on my bony knees are drained anaemic.

The distant *drringing* phone is getting close to insulting in my ears.

I should be out having sociable café cakes and cups of teas, planning giggly trips to movies.

I am staring at turquoise tendrils at my feet and thinking how aggravating that this carpet is merely laid on top of another one, that's of equal ugliness but more worn, poking out maroon around the edges of the room.

Nothing matches. It's not bothered me before.

The law says 'Furnished' must feature this and that. So here it is: a battered fridge that's hardly any colder than the air around me; an outsized wardrobe veneered with plastic; a one-ring Baby Belling in the corner.

The only thing here that seems to have a purpose is the briefcase, prepared for work on Monday, erect and almost keen where I place it on the formica, leg-splayed table in the centre.

For *Christ's sake*, someone answer that *bloody* phone!

Its *drrrings* cut short, at last. My head's a lead weight sinking down my body.

'*Allie.*'

An angry shout from downstairs says that the call's for *me*.

I can't cross the room fast enough. It seems my fingers don't have full control. The rattly yale keeps twanging shut.

Yank the door open; hear it crash against the wall behind me as I leap three stairs at a time. I'm at the phone. Too eagerly, I say, 'Hello?'

There is an infuriating pause while the *blip—bloops* in my ear confirm with aggressive impersonality that this is a pay-phone.

'Martin Bennett here.'

It's Dad! I grin. On Sunday nights I always do my phone call to him. He never normally calls me up. Even

163

so, his tone's the same: gruff, no time-wasting, like it's an obligatory work communication.

I sing out, 'Hello, Dad,' echoing under the plastic fluorescent hall light. 'How are you?'

There is silence on the other end of the phone.

I prompt him, 'Dad?'

'Well?' he demands curtly. 'What do you want?'

What do I want?! *You* contacted *me*! I brandish the heavy, distancing handset. Or, actually, since you ask, maybe . . .

'I'd like to meet.'

'Who?'

You of course.

Then suddenly I'm thinking, why, what for? Instantaneously countering that perhaps it shouldn't be to do with reason. How about, quite simply, it could turn out to be enjoyable. I sniff for strength the stale hall air. I think of somewhere that's anonymous, and equidistant from us both.

'Let's go to Bolton Abbey.'

There's more unnerving silence.

'Dad,' I blurt, 'I need to talk.'

Indeed? I sarcastically reprimand myself. *Start now, since talking's after all what phones are for.*

No, I meant in person.

It seemed the bus journey out from enmeshing streets and city terraces would take forever. I was sure I would be late. Now I wish I hadn't rushed. Without a jumper underneath, my thick grey mac, even though it's buttoned right up, only seems to trap in cold.

Standing waiting in the Bolton Abbey ruins, I won't admit disorganisation. I lean effortlessly non-chalant against a stone pillar that's crumbled at the edges. All around me is disintegrated austere grandeur.

Precarious half arches taper into sky. A crow flaps through a stained-glass window's skeleton.

I turn to face the open grassland. I see a heavily overcoated man. It must be Dad. He looks annoyed, the way his neck's skewered into his shoulders. He stride-stamps closer, his brows lashed maybe tighter than I've ever seen them.

I mean to call out cheeringly.

'Hel-lo, Dad.'

His head rears up.

I've dragged him all this way. I have to speak. About the weather? Or the journey here? Crass, stupid small talk.

'Dad,' I declare before I can catch myself, 'It's my job . . . '

Dad looks like he's shaking free from several other thought commitments.

'Your job,' he repeats stiltedly, more confused than I am.

'I'm not sure that it's, perhaps . . . ' I say, thinking: now I need a link sentence to take me to a different subject. But my mind's bogged down.

All the reasons for applying for the job still stand. It is in computers. They are the future. Start at the bottom. Establish a solid foundation. Build expertise slowly but surely. All these things, I know, Dad thinks sensible and proper. The boss likes me. The work's secure.

'But Dad, the petty bickering!'

His expression collapses into, *For Christ's sake – welcome to the real world!*

His eyes go blank and introvert. He snaps, 'It's a decent wage. You can't survive on air.'

Work problems are thrashing in together, making it impossible to explain *why* the stupid small things matter. And yet they don't. The sick metallic smell of discs, the snideyness about the tea rota – all of that is just the sandpaper that's grinding down my head. At **165**

9 a.m., I step on to the office nylon tiles, and I feel I have betrayed myself.

'Dad . . . ' My voice is treacherously warbling.

'I've made some wrong decisions.' Dad's staring suddenly at my eyes, not responding to the words. I see wide black irises encased in hazel, chocolate flecks. This concentration, on me, on what I'm doing and thinking, is what I must have wanted. So why am I feeling in a panic? I wish I could interrupt and say I wasn't serious – everything is *fine*.

His voice is careful. 'If the good outweighs the bad, then keep the job. If not, then leave.'

I thought he'd say I should stick it out.

I am immensely grateful and glad. And almost guilty. I'd like to make this into the casual walk I suggested.

I begin to walk along the muddied footpath that leads towards the river. He follows, unsure, as if he's drunk, or maybe scared. I rouse my cheerleading mood.

'Has the house sale gone through smoothly?'

A caring, chatty question, only it's like I've hit a mains pipe. It seems emotion will burst his face.

'It's right and proper,' he declares, trying desperately for gruffness, 'that you should want to know what happened between your mother and myself.'

No, Dad, you're wrong! I never asked on purpose.

'I anticipated that the time would come –' his hands are heavy by his side '– when you would want information.'

He has been preparing himself, all these years, for today. His mind is flicking crazy over everything he couldn't bear to think about.

He pulls one straggly sentence out.

'Three pregnancies . . . so quickly. They proved . . . a strain.'

Please stop.

'We thought the move to Withensty's . . . '

Something snaps inside him. He rages, 'I put a lot of work into that house!' Then furious silence; temples flickering pressure.

By hand, saving money, he laid the paving outside the back door himself. Mum stayed locked in a black infusing mood in *her* room. Dad couldn't keep his concentration on the job. A York stone slipped, on to his leg, levering him backwards, trapped. It must have been agonising pain. Phyll wouldn't let him move until she had – in playtime nurse's outfit, red-crossed towel on head – made him better. His eyes screwed shut. Blood seeped out where he bit his lip while Phyll administered a toilet-paper bandage to his leg.

The house has more importance to him than any ever should.

'Dad, how *is* the house sale going? What does Scarlet think?'

'Hmm . . . I haven't seen her, recently.'

I want to blurt out, *phone her*! But then his shutters would slam shut.

I can imagine how, out of self-destruction, by clinging to the house, he's done his best to drive Scarlet Barr away, in case that's what she really wanted. And then, today, because of how I was on the phone, he started thinking what I somehow needed – no, demanded, was an explanation.

What can I do?

I think of his desperate willingness to help me a few minutes ago, and how he can't do it for himself.

I think of his fight to construct a sea-kale healthy diet. I think of him crying under the plum tree when he'd been trying too hard to cope for too long.

'Dad, you've been a wonderful father.'

His head lurches back. His eyes circle in confusion. I suppose he can't think what he should reply. He gives up. His eyebrows hammer down with a sealing-off finality.

He mumbles awkwardly, 'Perhaps we've walked enough.'

He turns, wobbly, on the thin muddy path. He fumbles for his car keys.

'I suppose you'll want a lift,' he says, trying to get his eyebrows to lash together mock-severe, then adding quietly, 'I'd like to give you one.'

We are grown up. You don't have to be responsible for us anymore. Nor we for you. We can be friends.

■

I feel at last I can begin to change.

Today it is Dad's 50th birthday. Scarlet has invited us to celebrate it in a house she's borrowed.

Turned off a cottage-cluttered road, standing at a wrought-iron gate, I appreciate this red-brick, three-storey building for its neutrality.

Over lawn and plastic sun-chairs and clambering clematis, I can see through the tall rectangular window, my family.

I feel nearly giggly that I'm the last one here. I've always been so panicked-punctual before.

Although, I can't stop myself understanding more than makes me comfortable. Even through the silencing glass, I know Scarlet is instigating a scene that will make Dad comprehend that Phyll is an adult.

Scarlet's hand goes out, offering Phyll a cigarette. Dad responds on cue with an expression of mixed-up horror, while Max's tension towering behind shows resentment that Dad's attention is all on Phyll. Scarlet attempts to squeeze Max's shoulder, to draw him in. Max does not want *her* affection. He shifts angrily. Steel toe-cap crunches understated chic. Pink-tipped matches fly up in a tic-tacking wooden hail . . .

168   Normally I'd be anxious, rushing inside to

sort things out. From my distance at the end of the tarmac path, I shut my eyes and tell myself: it's up to them.

The purpose is to be here for Dad's birthday. *Celebration.* Staring defiantly towards the sky, I push the gate, which swings freely open.

But then I skewer my glasses hard on to my nose. I'm infuriated by this automatic self-preserving movement. I make the same hand *undo* my top, neck-clamping shirt button as I stride with what I want to be a cheerful gait towards the door.

Stepping into the room, I revel in its unfamiliarity. I stand on an oriental carpet.

'Hello!' I call out.

They swivel round, and the air fills with pleasure that is caused by *my* arrival. Scarlet and Phyll are dashing over, crying, 'Allie!'

Boa-constricted by Scarlet's unexpected hug and the force of Phyll's welcoming grip on my arm, I can scarcely believe I'm hearing that Max's 'All right?' is broken-voiced. And over Scarlet's shoulder, Dad, in a chintzy easy-chair, doesn't even move a jaw- or brow-muscle to stop pride flooding into his face.

I am overwhelmed.

I holler recklessly, 'Happy Birth—!'

Silence. The book in Dad's lap is yanked up in front of his body like a shield.

He wouldn't normally let us celebrate his birthday. Presents – inexpensive only! – were accepted grudgingly, and there would be *no* possibility of anything even resembling a party . . .

Scarlet, the guilty culprit, mumbles about going out to the kitchen to get the cake.

I am trying to cling my mind to a new freedom from duty concept, but a pressing down of obligation is forcing me to hustle Dad and Max and Phyll around the table.

Yet as well as irritation, I'm feeling blanketed by nostalgia.

This Quaker-style wood-stratted chair is as uncomfortable as our old bentwoods. The surroundings are irrelevant after all. We've fallen as a matter of course into our usual formation, me opposite Dad with Phyll on my right and Max on my left.

Our moods go into pre-set templates too. Phyll and Max and me tense up, apprehensive as Dad knuckles under his glasses the way he does when he's had another bloody awful day at work. Phyll begins to glower at me as if it's all *my* fault. The atmosphere's like we could expect burnt sausages any minute.

But then, his eyebrows become suggestive. Judging by the spark in his eyes, he's tripped back to beyond when Mum'd just left. The jaw creases that are suppressing his smile deepen.

He covers his face in his hands. With a single upwards movement, it seems he's pushed his glasses on to his forehead and ripped out his eyes.

Err! The trick of peeling back his eyelids!

We're regressed to when he used to do this when we were tiny infants. 'Errr! Dad, don't!'

Egg-shaped eyes of raw, pink, veiny flesh, pulsating like he's some beast out of a horror film.

'Dad, *don't*!' we squeal, spiralling to a specific peeled-eyelid hysteria that's embedded despite the years.

There's a jolting sound of crockery in the kitchen. Dad's covered his face and suddenly his eyelids are turned right way round.

Scarlet's coming in. We don't want to exclude her, but this is our secret silliness. We all face her with – hopefully – looks of innocent expectation. She has a cake: outsize silk ribbon tied around the circumference in a lavish bow; elegantly tapering bees'-wax candles.

Dad concentrates into a hunched defensive expression that says, *well if you lot feel you HAVE to do this then I will suffer it for your sakes*.

I refuse to accept the assault of Dad not wanting attention. I open my mouth – but Phyll's beaten me to it: 'Blow them out,' she cries. 'And make a wish!' booms Max.

Dad's look around at each of us, from me to Phyll to Max to Scarlet, is perhaps not even a millionth of a second, but it's like he has detailed the sinews of a rope that binds us together.

There is a lump in my throat that makes it difficult for me to swallow.

Max delves into his kitbag. Champagne!

For all his gravelly voice and extra height, I'd just seen Max as Max. As he gets into practised straddled cork-extracting position I feel I've lost something: Max miniature beside me walking up the lane collecting conkers. He is working to project casual confidence. Two lines from nose-bridge to cropped hair-line shimmer between the freckles. The rigidity of his grip on the bottle-neck makes his thumbs drained white with pushing effort.

The cork . . . is easing out . . . any moment . . . it will . . . blow —

Ker-BAM!

With actor-precision, exact in time, Scarlet's here with flute glasses catching the gushing, frothed Champagne, exciting to me for its unrestrained fizz alone, even before the taste and headiness.

'Cheers!' I hear.

Champagne fizzes my lenses, spotting my seeing with sugar-gluey alcohol. Bubbles burst and multiply on my tongue, seeming to rise up through the roof of my mouth, easing through my head.

Lying on a spare bed at the top of the house, I am just resting for a while. This attic room is pleasant, cosy even – so different from the ones of mine.

Downstairs, it sounds like Scarlet is getting lively again and ready for a second innings of the party.

I'm contented here fingering the bedspread, which is made of countless joined-up floral patchwork pieces.

Floating up the stairs is the sound of more popping corks and clinking glasses.

My head is doing a spinning movement that takes it round the sloping room and back again to somewhere nearby on the pillow. This ought to be too awful. But it's *not* the stretchy thing. It's Champagne relaxation.

I don't mind hearing life go on around me. It's of no consequence whether I get to sleep or not.

I let my body go about its ranges of sensations, which are not, I realise now, necessarily unpleasant. My arm swells. It knots into an alien shape and feel.

I know actually I *could* call out, and Dad or Scarlet or Phyll or Max, or all of them would come.

It's not that we struggled through in darkness, then drifted far apart and everything was pointless.

I am lulled by sounds of – of who? My family, my closest friends, their varied tones reverberating through the floorboards.

I feel vibrant.

I was woken early. The soft calling of a wood-pigeon drifted through the slightly open window of the attic spare-room. I experienced shock – where am I? – and grabbed my glasses from the sloped wicker chair beside the bed. The lenses' filth oppressed me. The frames blocked out sections of the patchwork cover, the curled metal bedstead, the stencilled wooden wardrobe.

I took the glasses off. The edges of the stencilled rose motif flickeringly multiplied. I commandeered my eye muscles. The rose gradually came clear.

Downstairs, I am standing in the front-room. The plastic and scratched glass that was my mask stays firmly in my trouser pocket. It is time for me to go.

I've withdrawn all my savings. I have given notice at my sensible lodging situation and my job. Everything is left in order.

I close the wrought-iron gate quietly behind me. Excitement turns my guts to butterflies.

The grass verge down the cottage-lined lane is dancing with daffodils. The smell of dew in the air makes me carefree dizzy.

This is only fifteen miles away from High Kirkby. It couldn't be more different.

Here, where the road bends away from houses, I can see the river, undulating fields of grazing cattle and gently waving crops.

I turn towards the station, which is like a toy-town version: the black-pitched roofed, white board waiting-room looks purpose-built to shelter just one person; the plank platform is raised by spaced piles of bricks which are wound around by foxgloves.

It's odd to think from here my destination could be anywhere.

The distant train is like a banner, fluttering round curves of track that have been dictated by the landscape.

Perhaps Paul Cragg is waiting for me. But that's not right, to run to him. Why would he be able to put me back together?

The train is nearer, solid now, mechanical. I can make out windows.

So, what am I doing standing watching when if I am to be on it I must run?

Maybe – in my subconscious – want to stay . . .   **173**

The train is slowing by the platform.

I can't believe my feet are hitting solid. All my senses are concentrated on the gap between the doors, which is already starting to reduce.

No use worrying about mathematical probability – leap, a leap of faith for sure, because the doors are whizzing fast to their conclusion. And yet, I'm through!

My body is a coiled-up spring released.

My fingers wrapped behind me grip on to plastic-coated metal. My feet dig for balance into ridged rubber flooring. I can hardly take it in that the arbitrarily seated scattering of passengers are all turned staring, direct at me, with applauding, open smiles. My eyes flick wildly from tweed-capped farmer to nylon-tunicked teenage shop-assistant to muddy-booted rucksacked rambler. My obsessed trajectory has been the complete focus of attention. And I know I should be blushing, except that all my blood's still taken up coping with my lungs.

I am brightly crimson now, but grinning too, so broad I think my mouth's got new dimensions. I lean against the window, feel it cool against my cheek.

Over there, several fields away, beside an oak, I think I see someone. The stance reminds me of Paul Cragg. I expect myself to somersault internally. His distant silence tells me, no more talking. It's time to shut down the voice – get on with living.

I've done it.

I'm going.

RATTLEBONE

Maxine Clair

'I love Maxine Clair's writing . . . She is a writer who should be read right now or folks will be missing out on something special' – *Terry McMillan*

'Her novel is perfect' – *Time Out*

'A vibrant, tender celebration of a black community on the brink of integration. Like the treacherous Missouri levee down the road, this deceptively slender novel is fit to burst with impatient passions and overdue tragedies' – *Observer*

BONES AND MURDER

Margaret Atwood

'Full of fun and invention, with an edge that cuts through preconceptions . . . an entertaining sampler of Atwood's cleverness and imagination'
– *Nicolette Jones, Independent on Sunday*

We hear how cooking undergoes a sex change, learn of alternatives to the happy ending or to *Hamlet* and listen to a reincarnated bat explain how Bram Stoker got *Dracula* all wrong. These wise and witty writings are pure Atwood – deliciously strong and bittersweet.

SNOW STORMS IN A HOT CLIMATE

Sarah Dunant

'Dunant ekes out the tension in a thriller that is comfortably shy of far-fetched and increasingly thrilling as the pages fly by' – *The Times*

When ballsy, bourbon-slugging Marla gets called to help out her friend Elly in New York, she finds herself ensnared in the dangerous twilight world of drug smuggling. Obsession, betrayal and revenge twist into an ever-tightening knot in this breathtaking psychological thriller.

FLESH AND BLOOD

Michèle Roberts

'A strong savour of Orlando about it – that is, of Woolf at her most flirtatious, bold and Colette-ish'
– *Lorna Sage, Independent on Sunday*

'The descriptive writing, the sheer joy of words . . . a wonderful feat' – *David Holloway, Daily Telegraph*

'An hour after murdering my mother, I was in Soho. That was where it began . . .' Freddy, a gawky, passionate adolescent is on the run. Through Freddy's fantasies – or are they realities? – we begin a journey into a world where history, memory and imagination meet.

SHADOW DANCE

Angela Carter

'Angela Carter's writing is pyrotechnic – fuelled with ideas, packed with images and spangling the night with her starry language. She brings the gift of wonder' – *Observer*

'In a modern-day horror story gleaming with perfect 1960s detail, she performs a double act, conjuring up just the right amount of Frankensteinian unease and perversion beneath the idiosyncratic business of relatively ordinary lives' – *The Times*

UNION STREET

Pat Barker

'Bold and imaginative . . . the dialogue is vivid, both bawdy and bitter' – *The Times*

'Powerful stuff . . . a remarkable first novel' – *Guardian*

'The long overdue working-class masterpiece' – *New Statesman*

'Gut-churning, nerve-shattering, heart-breaking and utterly imperative' – *New Society*

Books by post

Virago Books are available through mail order or from your local bookshop. Other books which might be of interest include:–

☐ Bones and Murder	Margaret Atwood	£5.99
☐ Union Street	Pat Barker	£6.99
☐ Shadow Dance	Angela Carter	£6.99
☐ Rattlebone	Maxine Clair	£6.99
☐ Snow Storms in a Hot Climate	Sarah Dunant	£5.99
☐ Flesh and Blood	Michèle Roberts	£6.99
☐ Free Love	Ali Smith	£7.99

Please send Cheque/Eurocheque/Postal Order (sterling only), Access, Visa or Mastercard:

☐☐☐☐☐☐☐☐☐☐☐☐☐☐☐☐☐☐

Expiry Date: _____   *Signature:* _____

Please allow 75 pence per book for post and packing in U.K. Overseas customers please allow £1.00 per copy for post and packing.

All orders to:
Virago Press, Book Service by Post, P.O. Box 29, Douglas, Isle of Man, IM99 1BQ.   Tel: 01624 675137.   Fax: 01624 670923.

Name: _____

Address: _____

_____

Please allow 20 days for delivery.
Please tick box if you would like to receive a free stock list ☐
Please tick box if you do not wish to receive any additional information ☐

Prices and availability subject to change without notice.